I0739123

WHAT BOOKS PRESS

AN IMPRINT OF

THE GLASS TABLE

COLLECTIVE

LOS ANGELES

ALSO BY A.W. DEANNUNTIS

Master Siger's Dream
The Mermaid at the Americana Arms Motel

THE FINAL DEATH OF ROCK-AND-ROLL

AND OTHER STORIES

A.W. DEANNUNTIS

WHAT BOOKS PRESS

LOS ANGELES

The author wishes to thank the editors of the following periodicals where these stories were first published: *The Evansville Review, Philadelphia Stories, Liquid Ohio, Lynx Eye, Los Angeles Review, Yemassee, First Class, Pacific Coast Journal, Short Stories Bimonthly, Luna Negra, CrossConnect, Spout, The Iconoclast, North Atlantic Review, Nite-Writer's International, Onionhead, Nuthouse, Mind in Motion, Kiosk, Cimarron Review, California Quarterly, Dog River Review and Coe Review.*

Publisher's Cataloging-In-Publication Data

DeAnnuntis, A. W. (Anthony W.)

  The final death of rock-and-roll : and other stories / A. W. DeAnnuntis.

    pages ; cm

  Summary: A compilation of fantastical short stories spanning thirty years of the author's writing career.

  ISBN-13: 978-0-9889248-4-0

  ISBN-10: 0-9889248-4-6

  1. Short stories, American. 2. Fantasy fiction, American. I. Title.

PS3604.E17 A6 2014

813/.6

What Books Press
363 South Topanga Canyon Boulevard
Topanga, CA 90290

WHATBOOKSPRESS.COM

Cover art: Gronk, untitled, mixed media on paper, 2014.
Book design by Ash Goodwin, AshGood.com.

THE FINAL DEATH OF ROCK-AND-ROLL

AND OTHER STORIES

for Chuck
and in memory of Russ Schneider

CONTENTS

AT THE BOOKSTORE, FOR EXAMPLE

I AM A MAN TO WHOM extraordinary things happen. Fabulous events transpire and I am at their center. The world revolves and I tremble in the slip-stream of the incredible. Remarkable moments flow through me as light passes through colored glass. I stand at the tremulous convergence of lines of force, tendrils of motion, wisps of cloudy and indistinct acts. If asked, I will tell you that the world exists because I exist. If it wasn't for me, nothing very interesting would happen.

At this juncture you are ready to read the words 'for example'. You are now prepared to consider an instance of the extraordinary events that shape, and are shaped by, my being. As you read this you say to yourself, "Okay, I have finished the prologue, now I will read about an example of the extraordinary things in this man's life." You have reached the point in this story where anticipation of the phrase 'for example' is all but a reflex. Undoubtedly this is the result of the accumulation of years of reading stories in which extraordinary events and remarkable scenes are presented with the inevitability of Christmas. Yours is, after all, a mind acutely trained to detect the subtlest clue, the most sophisticated hint, of exposition.

You are standing in the aisle of this large and well-lighted bookstore and have taken this volume from the shelf on a whim, a gust of curiosity, perhaps merely attracted by its brightly avant-garde cover. You have opened it to this story just as whimsically, perhaps perplexed by the exotic economy of its title.

It is possible, however, that you have chosen this book and this story because you have noticed an attractive woman (or man) standing further along this aisle, and you are anxious that person notices your cultivated taste in contemporary literature. As you read these lines you glance up as furtively as a teenager in a locker room, hoping you have been noticed by this desirable person.

And since you are crafty, accidentally you drop this book to the floor. Without looking around you quietly mutter a curse against yourself. Self-deprecating humor is a vital part of your arsenal of crafty devices deployed to attract those whose attention you desire.

In this gesture you notice that person is also holding a book. You recognize the author's name and remember that you have read reviews of this book with admiration. You remind yourself that because of the enthusiasm of the reviews you have intended to read this author's works. But regrettably, for all the reasons preventing you from reading the works of other, equally admirable authors, the work of this author remains among the confetti of brightly colored but unread spines surrounding you. Thus, even while you look forward to examples of the extraordinary events that transpire during my daily life, you have found yourself speculating about this person sharing your aisle in this bookstore.

Hurrah for you! You are displaying an ability only some humans possess; namely, the ability to carry on two distinctly different mental operations simultaneously. So intertwined are these two mental acts—anticipation of my examples of the extraordinary, and speculation concerning the intellectual tastes and artistic sensibilities of this person on your aisle—that to think one is already to be prepared to think the other. Though you may be unconvinced, you will have to trust me on this one.

But just then, that person looks up. For an instant your eyes are caught, your furtive glance is found out. Panic clutches your throat, you turn back to this page, desperately your eyes search for the phrase 'for example'.

For example, the description of a train trip through a foreign country that resulted in an unanticipated encounter with a long-lost friend would strike you as extraordinary. Or the recounting of a misadventure involving illicit drugs and the police would also strike you as remarkable. A chance meeting in a remote and desolate countryside with a relatively well-known pop star, perhaps also in a foreign country, would also fit your qualifications for an extraordinary moment. Even the chance discovery of a large denomination bank note on an infrequently traveled thoroughfare, especially if it happened in a foreign country, would be admitted into your realm of the extraordinary. In fact, while your eyes search this text for the phrase 'for example', a list grows in your mind of all the occurrences which would satisfy your expectations of an extraordinary event.

You are certain that if you glance far enough along in this text you will find the phrase 'for example'. And oddly, you almost hope that you do not, because discovery of that phrase would commit you to continue to read. Whereas, your preference is to study further the person at the other end of this aisle in this lovely large bookstore with subtly intellectual music playing in the background. But finally you look up and hope that person is no longer studying you, appraising you, waiting to catch your eye.

And you are relieved that person has turned away with their back to you, and so blocking your view of the cover of the book that person is reading, but also leaning one shoulder against the book shelves to give you ample opportunity to study their back.

And you do. You close this volume for a moment, your right index finger beside these words, and study unobserved the shape of shoulders, the curve of neck, the thickness of arm and waist, and—depending on thickness of garment—the style and panache of underwear encasing the curvature of hips and buttocks. You appraise the shape and thickness of thigh, the turn of calf, and even speculate on economic status suggested by style and brand of shoe. All of this you carry out quickly, indifferent to the possibility that just beyond the periphery of your eyesight, someone may be watching you.

Just then that person shifts and straightens and then begins to turn in your direction. Quickly you reopen this volume to the page still held by your finger, your eyes follow your finger, and at its end you read these words.

For example, several years ago I traveled alone in Europe on an extended vacation. An old friend had just married and was living with her new husband in Vienna. When she heard I was traveling she invited me to meet her new husband and stay for a few days, promising they would show me the sights. I had never been to Vienna and was glad of the opportunity to visit. But I was even more curious to observe the newly married couple. I had never met him, but she was a woman of some years acquaintance. And over those years had smoldered within my heart an unrequited desire. Profoundly voluptuous with abundant dark hair and a coquettish smile, she had featured in fantasies too prurient to describe, so that the joyful news of her marriage had left a sting of regret. This visit offered the opportunity to revisit these fantasies and perhaps finally put them to rest.

Because you are an acute reader of contemporary fiction you already suspect a tale of adultery cast against the backdrop of an exotic city, perhaps a series of night scenes in dingy rooms under unnatural light. You foresee all of this and pause. And then you look up.

That person is gone.

You return your finger to a place beside these words, you close this volume against your finger, and you sigh. You realize, of course, that this was the risk you took when finally you read the words 'for example'. Yet you are annoyed with yourself. You believe yourself sophisticated enough to carry out a bit of surreptitious surveillance within the civilized confines of a bookstore. This, at least, you can do. After all, you have had years to practice.

A wave of despair passes over you. Attention diverted, you remind yourself that once again you have let slip an opportunity. An opportunity for what, you question yourself. An opportunity to be swept up by the accidental, the impromptu, the extraordinary.

Cautiously you step to the end of the aisle, and as if you are not, you look along in both directions. But that person is utterly gone.

After a moment's regretful reflection you make a mental note of this page number and tuck this book under your arm. With one eye on the book shelves and the other on the aisles you begin a slow browse. Up one aisle and down another, noting all the books by all of the authors whose names you recognize and whose works you've always meant to read. In this fashion you reconnoiter the entire floor. And that person is not to be found. Now you are ready to accept the fact that person has probably—purchase or no—left the store. Enchanted within a cloud of despondency you wander over to the coffee bar.

When asked by the wait-person, you request a café-au-lait. Cheerfully the wait-person tells you the espresso machine is broken, so that person can only offer tea and American-style coffee. You ask for hot chocolate. That person glances at you once as if wondering who would order hot chocolate on a day like today and then begins to prepare it. The eyes of the wait-person are telling you things you never even wondered about. But happily your despondency insulates you from reflection. Besides, the wait-person at the coffee bar of a large bookstore is rarely a source of the extraordinary. So instead of engaging this person in a conversation, you glance around at the tables. A person reading a book is more interesting than a person serving coffee. Or in your case, hot chocolate.

Ceramic mug of hot chocolate in hand and this volume still under your arm you go to a small two-seat table that has not yet been cleared from its previous occupant. You would not have chosen this table so far from the sunny and popular windows but the place is crowded and it's the only table unoccupied.

After clearing a place for your hot chocolate and this volume you sit down. You sip your hot chocolate; it is very hot and sweet and you are pleased. Then you survey your immediate neighbors. The number of this page comes to mind, you open the volume and read these words.

Although it had been more than a year since I had last seen her, the sight of her from across the train station left me gasping. As if by some trick of the light, or perhaps our exotic setting, she seemed to have grown more alluring, more voluptuous and more desirable. When finally she recognized me she waved and approached as if floating across the bright pale floor. She greeted me with a vigorous hug, and kissed me as if we were old lovers. It was early in the afternoon, and she apologized that her new husband was at his office in a small industrial development a considerable distance away from the city. But she assured me that he would join us for a late dinner. I believe I smiled with unnatural brightness, and I am certain that I babbled like a school boy as she led me through the station.

It had been a long train trip and she invited me to have a drink at the station bar. Perhaps it was the effect of no longer moving, no longer being bumped and shaken in the train. Or perhaps it was simply the lack of lunch and then the two stiff drinks at the bar, but now as I sat across from her my desire bloomed. While we reminisced about friends at home, and then while she described her new husband, her new city and her new life, I felt myself tremble. The thrill of her presence was delicious.

When we finished our second drinks she mentioned that their apartment was not very far away and that we could take a cab. We rode very close together, the way her thigh rubbed against mine as our cab turned tightly in the narrow streets excited me. Dazed and a bit light-headed, I became increasingly confident that an extraordinary moment was approaching.

The apartment was large and well-decorated, almost luxurious, with tasteful and curious furnishing and thick overstuffed furniture between broad high windows which flooded the room with honey-colored light. I was hardly inside the door and had only just put down my bags when she suggested that perhaps after such a long trip I wanted to take a shower to freshen up and relax. In the meanwhile, she would prepare a light lunch. And afterward she would take me for a stroll around the neighborhood. The light in her eyes and the smile on her lips set the hairs on my head tingling.

Suddenly you feel a flush of relief. You now know where this description is going, and you believe you know how all of this will end. You congratulate yourself on your perceptive observations, you lean back in your chair, glance up from this page, take another sip of hot chocolate, and look around.

And there that person is.

You are so startled you are frozen in place. That person is sitting two tables away, and, judging by gestures, is preparing to leave. So a critical moment arrives. You have a decision to make. Will you as usual simply watch that person gather things, abandon the refuse of a quick snack and beverage, and then stand and walk away? Or will you finally abandon an old habit, born as much from timidity as by any respectful common courtesy, and put yourself forward. Perhaps follow as that person walks back along the rows of book shelves to the escalator, strike up a conversation, make a clever and amusing comment, and leave the confines of this bookstore in that person's company? You have only seconds to decide.

But of course there is no decision to make. You close this book without noting this page. Nonchalantly you set this book down without noticing the puddle of hot chocolate beneath. You sip quickly from your too-hot chocolate, take up your jacket and stand. From the periphery of your vision you notice when that person stands and when that person turns and when that person leaves the coffee bar. In a self-distracted manner you too move away from your table that now bears your half-empty mug of hot chocolate, this book, and the puddle of hot chocolate beneath. You drift in the direction that person has already taken, sorting through the clever comments you have stored in your memory.

Meanwhile the wait-person who first questioned your choice of hot chocolate watches you leave, and notices the mess remaining behind. With a damp towel in hand the wait-person goes to your table. In an instant that person recognizes that amidst the mess, this book has absorbed the spilled hot chocolate. The brown stain has colored the ends of these pages, the stain and the dampness have ruined this book and rendered it unsalable. The wait-person picks this book up muttering about the thoughtlessness of some people, carries it back behind the counter, and tosses it onto that pile of books similarly damaged and similarly ruined.

So, without a thought or a glance back, you have abandoned me and my story of extraordinary events. No longer curious about me, you are content to never know what extraordinary events have transpired in my life, or how they have affected me, or how I have interpreted their occasions and significance. And because this book is now ruined, no one else will ever know either.

But if you are fortunate, this story and the extraordinary events of my life are now among the least of your concerns.

MY HEART BLISTERS
LIKE A BROILED SAUSAGE

A COUPLE OLD AS MUD wobbles to my counter. He scowls like he's just stepped into dog shit, slaps his check down on the counter and slides it toward me, message-side up. In a phlegmy voice he growls, "What the hell's this supposed to mean?"

The back of the check reads, "You are dead already!" Of course I recognize my Marigold's arcane, Euro-trash scrawl immediately.

I say, "We choose our waitresses carefully from among the graduates of the finest waitressing school in Paris." I lean closer with my secret. "Many of them have read deeply in philosophy. I assure you this is obviously a philosophical statement."

The old woman at his side sneers. "Well if this is philosophy, somebody should tell her parents."

I respond, "They are as heartbroken as you are." The couple finally leaves and I'm relieved we'll never see them again. Neither them, nor their family nor their friends nor their professional colleagues. In fact, a whole army of greedy, gaping, chewing and drooling mouths now will never darken our door. I restrain myself from running to tell Ron the happy news.

My Tiger Lily moves in a nimbus of pale yellow light. Water glasses glitter in her presence, french fries glow at her touch. "Too late already so much."

She's come from one of those countries I've never heard of, and I'm not embarrassed to admit there are a lot of those. I assume her English will never get any better, which is just fine with me.

We all work together at the Kitchen Knook close to the shopping mall. I'm the late-shift cashier, a very demanding and responsible position, which is why I'm paid so little. Ron, the night manager, explains that the low pay discourages frivolous people who lack the drive and determination to take the job seriously. And he promises me that with another year of this responsibility I could go anywhere, do anything. Smiling he says, "Even president of, like, General Motors, or something."

Of course I'm impressed, even if I can't remember who General Motors is. I've told Ron we ought to have cool military uniforms. I remind him that people love uniforms, and they love to have their food brought to them by persons wearing uniforms. I explain to him that basically, this uniform-wearing is the wave of the future, and we need to be part of the future if we expect to succeed. I remind him that I watch the news, so I know what's going on. I tell him that from what I've seen, eventually all the people feeding us will wear uniforms and this will make us all really happy.

A young, attractive woman places her check on my counter, but she is not smiling. "You know," she says, "this sort of thing usually indicates serious psychological difficulties." On the back of her check my Little Petunia has scrawled, "The surface is without substance."

I respond, "We try to help those who are in difficulty."

"That may seem noble to you, but you should not inflict such darkness on those of us already entombed." A tear sparkles at the corner of her eye. She turns and leaves and my regret follows her like a thick snake.

My Buttercup waits tables from 4 PM until Midnight. What she does is what waitresses do, and her customers bring their checks to this cash register of which I am proprietor. They slide their checks across my counter accompanied by either a fist-full of cash, or a shiny credit card. We don't take checks, that's policy.

Our three other waitresses are named Camille, Ellen and Brandy. Hoping to pump up their tips, each writes little messages on the backs of their checks. Ellen is in law school, so she just writes "Thanks so much!" with a little diamond at the bottom of the exclamation point. Maybe she should change it to a dollar sign. Brandy writes, "Have a Good Day," and puts smiles in the middles of the "O"s. The horror is that she earnestly means it, so I tremble at her glance. But Camille is the worst. Camille writes, "Smile, God Loves you!" and she puts little hearts to dot the "I" and at the bottom of the exclamation point, and in place of all of the "O"s. It must take her ten minutes to draw the thing out. But my Squash-Blossom is different. Where others are mesmerized by what they believe, she sees all the way down.

"Stop touching yourself and start touching others," is written quirkily on the check slid onto my counter by a young man whose acne will be with him until he's collecting Social Security.

He says, "Woman these days are so fucked up."

I shrug. "Estrogen's been leaking into the water supply."

His eyes get large. "You're shitting me?"

"Drink bottled water," I say. "It's the only way to be safe."

My Rose-Blossom always shares her shift with at least two of these other waitresses, along with a revolving door of dark, foreign-looking busboys who pass through so fast I never learn their names. So we have four waitresses for a three-waitress staff. Ron makes up the schedule. He says the task will make him crazy. Apparently, doing the schedule is the hardest thing he's ever done, even from high school, figuring out how to cover from day to day, week to week. He begs me to pick up the bus-tray whenever I can. These women will drive me nuts, he says, and I'm sure that would be a short trip. But I remind him that busing tables is beneath the responsibilities of the cashier, who must handle money. After all, what is more diseased-ridden in our society than cash, filthy cash?

Ron does not like me and never agrees with anything I say, think, or do. But he does not want to hire another cashier. His cashiers tend to very cunningly steal, and he tells me I'm the first in half a decade not frantically robbing his place blind. All Ron wants to do is sit in the back-office at the computer downloading porn from the internet onto cd's he takes home with him every night and does god-knows-what with thereafter. I'm too nauseous to ask.

"The brain atrophies before the penis," is followed by a smiling sun-face with X's over the eyes. The middle-aged guy belonging to this check grins as he leans across the counter. "I just took my pill," he whispers, "and I've got a woody like a sequoia. What time does she get off?"

"She doesn't," I assure him. "Our evil manager keeps her shackled in the basement. He's the only one gets to see her."

He frowns sympathetically. "Any little thing I can do to help?"

In fact I keep all of these complaints from Ron. He likes my Little Dove even less than he likes me. He thinks she thinks about him. If it wasn't for the fact that she can carry six filled platters in the middle of a rush, she'd have been long-gone. At closing I count the register while she helps clean up. I lose count every time I look up to see her bending over. I lose count a lot, so this usually takes the rest of the night. Ron comes over to me after firing another busboy. He likes to keep in practice. "Stupid little shit," he says looking at nothing in particular, and it takes me a second to realize he's not talking to me. "Any of your creepy friends need a job?"

I tell him my creepy friends are all over-booked. I tell him it seems like people will only hire the really creepy ones. He looks hard into my eyes. "You don't like this job, do you?"

"I love this job," I say. "I gave up being General Motors just to work here."

He looks at me a moment and then he smiles. "My bet is you're going to be here a good long time."

I ask, "Is that a promise?" I finish counting, or actually just give up and write down the amount on the slip that I already know is supposed to be in the register.

"Oh yeah," he says, "that's my promise to you!"

As he walks away I say, "Thanks! Mom will be so pleased."

I time my departure to follow her out the door. Half a block from the restaurant I say, "Listen, you have to stop writing that shit on the checks. People get upset. They say things. They think things."

She shrugs without turning. "Bargains you cannot see but feel. Too much there is without. Shit money, what the fuck."

I say, "It seems they are not grateful for your subtle generosity."

"Appetite is the burden on my shoulders, gratitude is space in the air." She has gorgeous shoulders.

I say, "If you don't like gratitude you should be happy every day."

Finally she turns, her arrogant frown thrills me. "Happiness is the belief you will not die."

"Do you ever have a good time?"

She stops at the corner, her bus is already pulling up. She shrugs as she brings a token out of her pocket. Climbing the steps she does not turn. "Misery is underrated."

The doors fold closed, her sweet butt framed sweetly in the folding bus-door windows. Nothing left for me to do but sigh, which I do louder than the bus.

Two women. Young, secretary-types. The taller, older one slides the check toward me like we're conspirators and this is grade school. On the back of the check my Dumpling has written, "A penis in the hand - better two in the bush."

"How was your meal today?" I ask with the blandest look I own.

"Funny," she says, and the two leave giggling. I spend the next ten minutes figuring.

After closing, my Nightingale leaves without a glance back. I hustle to catch up, pull up just behind her right shoulder. Her profile fills me with something I cannot name.

"Tell me; was it the Freud that didn't sit well, or the Kafka?"

With her firm, long-legged gate she steps on the gas. I hustle double-step to keep up. "Why these things they have they?" She turns to face me without losing a step, her grin vicious and wise. "You!" And she says, "You!"

At the corner she turns. A guy is just getting out of a cab. She strides faster, has her hand on the closing door, slips inside and is gone, all before I can say, "Me! Me! Me!"

Two little girls, maybe twelve years old between them, timidly place their check and cash on my counter. On the back I read, "Death is your friend!" I shove the cash back toward them.

"Hey!" I say kind of loud and I'm smiling. "It's your lucky day. You're lunch was free! Hope you enjoyed it. Come back again soon!"

I'm relieved when the little girls turn to each other and smile. The one girl says, "Thanks," as she grabs the cash. The other says, "Yeah," and they're laughing together before they reach the door. And I'm relieved nobody is making a big deal if they overheard.

An hour and a half later and it's slow. To my Dandelion I say, "We have to talk."

I take her by the elbow to lead her to the back. She shrugs me off, gets to the office door before I do, stands arms folded across her generous chest and watches me approach like a hot dog watches mustard. I stand as close to her as I can without fainting. "Please leave the kids alone. If you aren't about to say something nice to a kid, just shut up. How about it?"

The fire in her black eyes roasts my scrotum no matter which way I turn. "Can you can't there say out of it what the fuck?" When I don't answer she sneers. "Pot- licker," she says and then she moves past me like I'm a can of dead flowers. People want to know why I hate my life, I shouldn't need to point.

Back at the register, Ron comes over with a smile like his whole face's been shot with botox. He calls out, "Brandy, cover the register a minute?" He signals me to follow and we walk back to the storeroom. He flicks-on the light and closes the door behind us. He paces back and forth smile gone and looking like he's been constipated for a month. Watching him move is about to wear me out. I sit down on a case of catsup bottles. Finally he looks like he's decided something and he steps close and leans forward. Real quiet he says, "We have a problem." He freezes then, stares into my face like whatever I do next will twist my future permanently. So I do nothing. "We're missing a can of mayonnaise," he says. Then he watches me like by knowing this I will now change into something.

"A whole can of mayo, you say?" I squint and dip my head as if overwhelmed by the remarkable and pretending I know what he's getting at. I ask, "Any ideas?" Because I don't like this having-to-think forced upon me. I'd rather that it sneak up on me, like a toothache or Death, until finally I'm forced to do something about it, but all along I've already been sort of dealing with it in the background.

With cultivated inscrutability he says, "One or two," and then takes a step back, "one or two." He sits on stacked boxes of canned soup and sighs, rubs his hands together and then along the tops of his thighs. The aura of defeat hovers about him as miasmal as a fart.

To move things along I ask, "One of the gallon cans?" I'm incredulous because it is incredible, and I need to be certain before I continue with this thinking-thing. He nods.

"And you're sure it's not misplaced?" I ask. "Because you looked everywhere?"

Silence in this case is assent.

"Well," I say still not grasping the magnitude of our situation, "it wasn't like it was a can of the good stuff. Can't be more than a few dollars a can. I mean, we'll make it up."

Suddenly he looks at me in a way that I had never expected him to look. As if his face was a set of tools and this expression was just not included. "You don't get it, do you?" Bitter suspicion tightens his eyes. "Can you be so fucking self-centered and naive?" He stands, slowly steps forward to bring his face right up to mine so that I have to lean back. "This isn't just about the fucking money. It isn't even about any fucking principles. The question I can't answer is; why? And even worse; how?" His own suspicion turns to incredulity. "Pick up one of those fucking cans, go ahead. How you going to sneak one of those out of here? Where the fuck you going to hide it? How you going to carry it so nobody guesses? What kind of fucking bag you going to put it in so nobody says, hey, where you taking that gallon of fucking mayo?"

Before I can venture any stupid guesses he says, "And why? How much goddamn mayo can one family eat, for Christ sake?" He begins to pant, his voice is getting louder, and I'm wishing he brushed his teeth more often. "You can't put this shit on goddamn breakfast cereal, for Christ sake!"

Ron looks around the floor like he's surrounded by scorpions. "And if somebody's snatched the mayo, should we maybe put an armed guard on the tuna?" His face has become very red. Ron's easily in his mid-thirties and at his age I'd be careful about cardiacs and strokes. But he's throwing caution to the wind. "I defy anyone to explain to me why any normal human being would steal a gallon of goddamn mayonnaise!"

Who could imagine Ron is a passionate philosopher? But he's already given-up trying to find anything out from me. He's turned and is already reaching for the door handle. So with hardly a twitch he's opened the door. And there stands my little Flesh Bulb.

She's looking a bit cowed though she's easily a head taller than Ron. "Chair hut token, leech, faucet already." Ron stares up at her a long time. My Sweet Onion cannot return his look. He steps around her and returns to the restaurant. She stands another moment looking at the floor and then she returns to the restaurant. And me? I'm still sitting on my ass, Brandy covering the register for me, and I'm waiting for the noise of this head-thing to stop, so much like a blender running filled with steel screws.

A priest comes to my register smiling, slides his check toward me with his cash. I see her handwriting and tremble. I turn it over to read, "Sleep with God!"

The priest says, "Your staff has a rare and subtle sense of the world behind the mask. I shall return often."

Panic grabs my throat. I suppress the scream and manage to mutter, "That would perhaps not be wise." The priest's smile disappears as his eyes get large. Leaning closer I say, "Our manager is a Satanist and he would say anything to corrupt you." I drop my voice to add, "He would even lie to you."

The priest is about to turn. I touch his sleeve and add, "Pray for our souls." The door closes and he never looks back.

About a second later Brandy steps up smiling. "Let me know if you need me to cover for you." Her voice is so bright I want to put on sunglasses.

"That's generous of you, but I can't possibly burden you with this enormous responsibility." I pull another girly magazine from the rack and lean back as I open it.

When I look up again I'm surprised to see Brandy still standing there. She cranks her smile up another level. "I hear Ron's got you on some kind of inventory duty or something. About the tuna, I mean. It's a little slow today. Maybe I could give you a hand."

Now I'm looking for the hidden camera. These places always have hidden cameras even though they usually don't work, but if we have them, they must be really well-hidden. So I ask, "Did you wait on that priest?"

Brandy demonstrates a panic entirely out of proportion to that question, which relieves me completely. "No," she says, "that's what's-her-name had his table. Why?" As if she doesn't know. "Did he complain?"

"No, worse. He was so impressed he threatened to bring all his priest-friends here. Does that make any sense to you?" I look at her real hard, a sort of highlight and underline to the point.

She turns and scans the room as if help might arrive any second. She shrugs before she turns back again. "I guess some old guys find her type charming. Don't ask me; old guys are always so obvious." There's nothing to that with my name on it so I let it drift. After another minute she drifts too, and I'm relieved.

A withered and old woman about four feet tall staggers to the counter, slides her check across and says, "What the hell's this shit?" My Little Cauliflower has written, "Sex is death."

"Words to live by," I say hoping that if I don't look at her she'll evaporate.

"Know anybody needs to get laid, give 'em this." Then trembling, she scribbles a phone number at the bottom of one of the take-out menus stacked on the counter. She doesn't wait for me to answer, but it takes her four minutes to walk to the door. When she's gone I fold up the menu and shove it into my back pocket. I know that one never knows.

A heartbeat later Ron's standing beside my shoulder. "You know who that is?" "Don't know who she is, but I know what she wants."

"She's maybe old and crazy but she's rich as they come."

"Then, here!" I say and pass him the menu. "She's waiting for you to call."

He looks at the menu with widening eyes. "You shitting me?"

"Would I shit you?"

He grins. "That's why I let you work here." He walks away lips muttering the phone number like he expects to remember it.

Walking behind my gorgeous Petunia as she makes her way to her bus I say, "Your English is getting so much better."

Walking fast she shrugs without turning. "So much there already what so little and already so little."

Perhaps my little Artichoke is a secret poet. Her way with words is so elegantly awkward. Or perhaps she simply speaks as she thinks. Thinking and speaking so rarely coincide, but perhaps my Apricot Jelly has discovered some secret. And perhaps if I'm earnest and determined she'll share that secret with me. We reach her bus stop and I'm about to peel off toward my apartment but she turns to me. "Every day is coffee, how is that, how is that."

I'm stunned. No words, her eyes are black icicles in bright sunlight. And for the first time ever, she smiles. Her teeth are bad but her smile is brilliant. By the time my brain remembers I have a mouth and the muscles in my jaw unlock, she's already climbed the steps to the bus and has gone. When I get home I make a note on my calendar, it's that sort of thing.

One night we're really busy, a convention or something, I only find out after the fact, but ninety percent of our customers are female and almost all of them are young.

For the entire evening rush, Ron's running in one direction and looking in the other.

Beaming with his natural-born idiocy, he can't get to these tables fast enough. He's even carrying platters and busing tables, an explosion of activity that demands to be commemorated with a photograph it's so unlikely. It's Brandy's day off, just Camille and Ellen and my Sweet Plantain, and we're all stunned by Ron's enthusiastic participation, though for different reasons and to different degrees. Ron's one of those hiding-managers; don't bother him unless the register's short or there's blood on the floor. My little Star-Light maneuvers around Ron like he's a pile of dog shit. Even Camille finds his participation remarkable, so she makes a remark.

"What's he doing here?"

"As little as possible."

"Doesn't he know even how to carry dishes?"

"Like the rest of us, he knows as little as he can get away with."

"Something's going to happen," she says.

"Something always does." I know I'll be proved right, but I'm surprised at how soon.

The collision happens when I'm not looking, but the sound wakes even the comatose. The sudden stream of venom from my little Buttercup's sweet lips is terrifying Ron shields himself with his server tray. Fortunately, my Sugar Cube has reverted to her mother-tongue, so no one understands what she's saying, but none of us needs a translation. Women at the tables giggle and point, terror and embarrassment alternate in Ron's eyes like lights on a billboard. My little Lollipop's pale face is red as a sunset, and then to all of our surprise, big, bright tears appear in her eyes. Its then my heart shatters with the last dropped glass.

In the next instant Ellen appears with broom and dustpan muttering about lawsuits. My little Nectarine is sobbing, tears glide down her cheeks, and I struggle to resist running over to lap them up with my tongue.

But Ron suddenly recaptures his self-importance and sense of disproportion and explains to my Love Doll that she's fired.

Without a thought beyond a pointless hope to spare my little Pop-Tart any more embarrassment I decide to tell Ron that I quit, and then describe to him how deep into Hell I know he'll fall. And I'm ready to do this. And I promise myself I'll do this, just as soon as I can step away from the register.

But somehow my hands have become cramped around the edge of the counter. Somehow they've escaped my control and have conspired to hold onto the counter-edge. Do they know something I don't? Do they understand something that has completely escaped me? Do they recognize something about me that I ignore at my own peril?

Have they learned something from working here that I've forgotten, or worse, never even recognized? Just clamped onto the edge of the counter, and I can't make my hands relax.

Suddenly and to my surprise Ron's standing immediately beside me. "You put up with this shit every day, you deserve a raise." And then he mutters into my ear a number.

He's breathing hard so I'm pretty certain he's serious. Frozen by greed and cowardice perhaps, my left hand, the faithless hand, the treacherous hand,

the hand that can't be trusted, devious, cynical and cruel remains gripping
the counter. I call upon my trusty right hand, but clearly it has entered
into a conspiracy with the left. My hands in remorseless grip of the counter
are listening to Ron, and they like the sound of his number. My hands are
thinking about my landlord and my checkbook, and how good it feels to wrap
themselves around a mug of cold beer. And thinking this they begin to think
how they would miss all this. So my devious, treacherous hands betray me.
As they so often have in the past, they do as they wish and not as I want. My
hands are content to watch my little Pudding-Cup tearfully gather her things,
exchange her apron for her overcoat and then walk to the door. But worst,
most dreadfully, most terribly, my hands smile derisively as my Tulip-Blossom
steps out the door without even a single, vicious glance back.

When Brandy comes in the next day she makes it clear to Ron she believes
my Succulent Rasinette was dealt with too harshly. Ron fires her before her
coat's off. She looks hard at me as she leaves, but no tears for her and tougher
than I'd guessed. By the dinner-rush two new waitresses are plying our
victuals; women who've been yelling at cooks and filling water glasses since
Regan was president. A reassuring stability has emerged, refreshing in its
inconsequentiality.

My hands are ecstatic with money play, but my heart remains unemployed.

HEMINGWAY'S DENTAL HYGIENIST

ERNEST HEMINGWAY, the famous fruit-fly collector, was cleaning one of his favorites, a bottle-nose named Scotty he'd picked up in El Salvador in '47, when his telephone rang. The hurricane three days before had passed just south of Key West, making a mess of his collection. He could look forward to days of cleaning and buffing. This thought made him more surly than usual, and he knew it. And as usual he'd been drinking.

He held the receiver between shoulder and ear. Cigar clenched tight in yellow and rotted teeth, his beard made a hissing sound against the mouthpiece. "Whadyay want?"

Silence except for heavy breathing. Hemingway was short on patience today.

"Open up or hang up, doesn't matter which," he said.

"I need your help," the words came slowly, smoothly. The voice was female, the color of good bourbon and he saw all curves and golden curls.

"I bet you do," he said.

"It's my husband," she said choking back tears, "he's such a jerk."

"Husbands usually are. What do you expect me to do?"

After a long pause she whispered breathlessly, "Kill him."

"That's all?" Hemingway's laughter was loud and harsh. He removed the cigar from his lips, leaned back in his rocking chair. "Sweetheart, if I killed every husband every wife ever asked me to I'd be more popular than beer."

"Please, Mister Hemingway, you're the only fruit-fly collector I can trust."

"Call me Papa."

"I can't."

Hemingway surveyed the collection around him. "All right," he said, "just give me a where and when."

"Midnight. At the end of the pier by Willy's Steakhouse."

"How will I know you?"

"At the end of a pier at midnight? Trust your instincts."

"Blondes," Hemingway muttered when the line went dead. "What is it with blondes and murder?" He looked up at the clock and realized it was nearly time for his dental appointment.

Hemingway never went to a dentist. He was embarrassed to open his mouth in the presence of others. He rationalized the neglect of his dental hygiene on the grounds that the pain and infection strengthened him, revived and challenged his endurance, the pain of gradual decay purged him of weakness and indecision. The women he slept with agreed he was okay in bed but his mouth smelled like an old fish-tank.

But now his thirty-second molar was nearly gone and a piece of broken enamel had caused an infection that was poisoning him. So for the first time since the Army he would go to the dentist.

He popped seven Sen-Sens as he stepped through the office door.

The dentist's name was Dr. Frank N. Stein. Dr. Stein walked past his receptionist and shook Hemingway's hand. "You know, you look a lot like Ernest Hemingway the writer."

"And I expect you get a lot of monster jokes."

Dr. Stein was just slightly taller then Hemingway. He cloaked his face in boredom and said, "Okay, let's hear yours. But I'll bet you ten dollars I've already heard it."

"You got me wrong. Why should I joke? I'm just a sucker for literary allusions."

Dr. Stein touched his fingers lightly along Hemingway's jaw. At the touch of the dentist's fingers, his jaw clamped shut. Dr. Stein did not appear to notice. He signaled to his beautiful hygienist assistant. "Set him up for a full exam."

The hygienist led Hemingway to a side office, motioned toward the dental chair.

When he leaned back he felt his neck lock. But he couldn't keep his eyes off the blond hygienist. Tall and broad-chested, narrow waist, dimple cheeked and green eyed, she moved like a willow in a mild breeze. She leaned forward to attach his bib, he watched her heart-beat pulse at her throat.

Dr. Stein appeared suddenly beside her. "What's all this then, eh?" He shouldered the hygienist aside and pried Hemingway's lips apart, pushed a heavily gloved finger along his gum line. His finger probed along the outside of his teeth in a way that Hemingway suspected was sexual. As hard as Dr. Stein tried, he could not force Hemingway's jaw to open further.

Annoyed, Dr. Stein straightened, pushed back the reflector from his eye. "Please, Mr. Hemingway, from what I've seen you have serious dental disease. You belong in the equivalent of a dental emergency ward. But you are here now, and so are we, so let's get going." He tried Hemingway's jaws again. Still frustrated, he filled a needle with some pale blue liquid. "This should make things easier." He peeled Hemingway's lips back and pushed the needle deep into his jaw.

It was as if a white hot wire had pierced Hemingway's neck to the back of his head. Dr. Stein did the same to the other side of his jaw. The pain was horrifying, it was wonderful. When Hemingway finally began to breathe again there was a half-smile behind his shaggy grey beard. In a few moments, his jaw dropped completely out of his control as he farted loudly.

"There," Dr. Stein said, "now I think we can begin." The beautiful dental hygienist grinned.

For the next two hours Dr. Stein and his delicious assistant mauled the interior of Hemingway's mouth. They scrapped and drilled and cut and sewed. They drilled and filled and filed and blasted. Puss and blood was everywhere. All three combatants were drenched in sweat, the hygienist most fetchingly with blond curls sweat-plastered about flush cheeks and burning eyes. Hemingway's mouth glowed with pain, his jaw muscles ached from constant pressure. It was wonderful. For a moment he wondered why he'd avoided it.

As a finale, sweat-soaked Dr. Stein gave Hemingway a course on the use of dental floss. "It's clear, Mr. Hemingway," the breathless dentist monotoned, "you have come to me in such distress because you never learned to floss properly. But I have showed you how it is done, so go and do likewise, every morning and every evening, and we will never need to see each other again."

"Flossing is for faggots." Hemingway's jaw was completely numb, when he spoke his lips flapped trailing spittle.

Dr. Stein's eyes glared angrily. "You have stared at this poor woman's breasts for the last two hours and if I hadn't taken a special concern for your condition I would have thrown you out of my office with nothing but a dirty towel." The hygienist stood behind Dr. Stein smiling. "Promise me you will floss at least once every day."

Hemingway's jaw fell open, crystalline stands of drool trailed from the corners of his mouth. "Fuck flossing."

"Suite yourself, Mr. Hemingway. Pay the girl on your way out. Cash only, please, I loathe personal checks."

"You can tell from faggots, they've got good teeth." By then the dentist and the hygienist were gone.

Hemingway stood brushing pieces of blood-soaked cotton from his clothes. The floor, he realized, was covered with them. The receptionist smiled as he approached. She offered him a basket of mints. He grabbed a handful, stuffed several into his mouth, paid her in cash and headed for the nearest bar; Philly's near the marina.

Hemingway drank bourbon with beer-chasers at Philly's, until he got tired of answering questions about his mouth. It kept falling open and he couldn't close it without using his hands. And he drooled. Eventually he bought a bottle of bourbon from the bartender and took it home. He could drink alone good as anybody.

Back in his room he sat in the chair beside his bed. After a few more drinks he fell asleep. He dreamed he was in a small boat in the middle of the ocean in the middle of the night. In his dream there was an enormous fish tied to the side of the boat and sharks were chewing on it. Hemingway kept hitting the sharks with his paddle, but the sharks just laughed and made fun of him, told him he was useless and old. In the dream Hemingway became sea-sick and depressed.

He awoke in a darkened room. The sun had set and street lamps in the distance glimmered through sea-mist casting yellow cones to the street. The fruit fly collection glittered neatly on the table. He glanced at the clock; already ten-thirty. He showered quickly, put on his loudest patterned shirt, stuffed himself into duck pants that smelled of dead fish. He shoved the rest of the mints he'd collected from the dentist's receptionist into his mouth. Beard still dripping from the shower, he slung a tan sports-coat over his shoulder and took a cab to Willy's pier.

A nimbus of yellow street light surrounded the front door to Willy's bar. Beside it and set several feet back in the shadows, a wooden arch framed three wooden steps leading down to the foot of the pier. At the far end of the pier a bright overhead light illuminated a single red-and-white gasoline pump. Hemingway took several steps along the pier before he saw her, poised standing in the shadow of the gasoline pump. An orange eye moved up and down beside her face. On a breath of wind he recognized her Havana cigar.

As he approached she stepped toward him. "You've come."

"Another minute looking at you and I will." He laughed quietly, his jaw flapped, his drool glistened in the moonlight.

"I never was much for sexually-oriented humor," she said coolly. "But you look better than you did this afternoon. Or maybe it's the light that's flattering."

The light was wrong but that was all right. The dental hygienist, but no longer dressed for the profession. In fact, hardly dressed at all.

"So, it's like that, is it?" Hemingway asked.

She smiled. "He's my husband. Now you see why I want him killed?"

"Fair enough. But what's the pitch? And what's in it for me?"

She paced a small circle under the lamp-post and spoke to the waves slapping the pilings. "To answer your last question first, pride of achievement and money. Answering the first gets complicated and takes time."

"You have a name?"

"Is it important?"

"I like to know the name of the party picking up the tab when I do a killing."

"Naming names won't get us where we want to go."

"But at least we'll know where we're at. Besides, you've got the advantage, you already know mine."

"For the time being, why not just call me Mrs. Stein?"

"I already know a Miss Stein, and you two wouldn't get along at all. On second thought, maybe you would at that."

"Dancing is not your style, Mr. Hemingway. And my feet are beginning to hurt." She drew on her cigar, pale blue plumes of smoke trailed arabesques beside her face.

Hemingway grinned. "My feet are getting tired, too. Suppose we sit down."

When he sat he let his legs hang over the edge of the pier. He patted a spot beside him. "Sitting together promotes candor."

Mrs. Stein hesitated. When she sat she drew again on her cigar and then she blew the smoke in his direction. "You asked why I want him killed."

Hemingway shrugged. "Maybe now I don't want to know. Maybe knowing will spoil it for me. Maybe all I need to know is that you'll pay me to do it. And maybe I'd better not need to know any more than that."

For the first time, Mrs. Stein smiled. "You surprise me, Mr. Hemingway. I suppose I never expected such clear-eyed delusion." With a shimmy of her tight skirt she moved closer to him. "Believe me, if I told you my reasons you would dispose of him eagerly. Let's leave it at that."

Hemingway grinned. "You're a gorgeous lunatic. You have natural flair, probably you were born for it. Anyway, you're a lunatic if you think I'll kill a man just because you tell me he's been bad."

"But the way he treated you today!" Mrs. Stein said with earnest surprise. "He enjoyed it. Didn't you notice the brutal zeal, the ruthless enthusiasm of his attack? He performed procedures on you he hasn't used since he was an intern. That was dental surgery without anesthesia. At the end of that session I knew you were the man to do what needed to be done."

Hemingway shrugged. With a grin and an extended hand he said, "Can I have a drag from your cigar?"

Mrs. Stein smiled as she passed to him. For a moment their fingers touched. Hemingway filled his barrel chest, taking the smoke deep into his lungs. When he exhaled the grey cloud seemed to billow around his head. Then he tossed the cigar out over the black ocean, where it fell with a splash. Hemingway grinned shyly. "I hate when dames smoke cigars."

For a moment Mrs. Stein seemed impressed.

"All right," Hemingway finally said. "I'll do it. But I have conditions."

"And should I guess the conditions?" She smiled in a way that made Hemingway's teeth ache. He liked it.

"Let's talk money now, and we'll get to the other stuff later."

"Five thousand now, and another five when it's done." Her upper lip curled on the word "done" in a way that left Hemingway dizzy.

After a moment he said, "Too much."

Mrs. Stein's smile disappeared.

"I don't kill husbands for pleasure or profit; I do it as a duty. There's hardly one that couldn't use killing. Yours is not exceptional. Except for his choice of wives."

Hemingway could see the change in her eyes, like a line of clouds parting to reveal the sun. "And don't worry," he continued, "I don't care why you're with him. So that's my offer; a hundred bucks here and now and we're even."

He could have been home polishing his fruit-fly collection and getting slowly, quietly and thoroughly drunk. Instead he sat at the end of a dock in the middle of the night with the most gorgeous woman he'd seen since Paris in '45. The question is not whether life gets worse, only in what ways.

Hemingway watched Mrs. Stein debate with herself while she studied him. Still unresolved she said, "And what are the conditions?"

"Like I said, a hundred bucks now. And you meet me after."

"Where?"

"First tell me where your husband is."

"At his office," Mrs. Stein said, and her expression soured. "Recently he hired a temp for some clerical work. She comes in Wednesday nights to answer the phone and do some filing. She and my husband are playing kissy-face in the examination chair right about now." She turned to face the ocean giving Hemingway the best profile he'd had in years. "I may be a fool but I'm not blind. That's why I'm here."

"And how long will he be there?"

Mrs. Stein sneered. "Oh, if I know my man, not very."

Hemingway felt the hair on his neck rise. He stood and Mrs. Stein stood with him. "Then I better get going. Suppose I hold the money." He held out his hand.

Mrs. Stein smiled. The smile reminded him of a grade-school teacher he'd lusted after for an entire summer back at a camp beside a lake in Michigan. There was a small piece of damaged flesh between two of his teeth. With his tongue he tortured it as he watched her rummage through her purse until his eyes began to tear. "Here," she said handing the bill to him.

Hemingway grasped the bill, but she held onto it. With a tug she fell lightly into his arms. She brought her face close to his, he inhaled her aroma of antiseptic. When she kissed him her lips pressed hard, and then harder. For a moment Hemingway thought his gums would begin to bleed again. The pain was brilliant. Suddenly her tongue, thick as a kielbasa, pushed past his lips. He felt himself swoon. He stepped back, his heel touched the edge of the pier. He took deep breaths. "Let's save the tongue-wrestling for when the job's been done."

"Where will I meet you?" Her eyes appeared to glow and the tone of her voice offered a preview of what he should expect.

"About two miles above the peninsula along Route 9 there's a roadhouse.

Quiet place, good food. The owner's an old pal who owes me a favor." Hemingway stepped past her with his fists clenched. It was the toughest three steps he'd ever taken. He stopped then and turned. The overhead light was behind her. Her silhouette was a sinuous wisp of dark smoke. The light passed through her clothes as if they weren't there. "Don't bother to show up before eleven," he said. He could hardly contain the tremble of his voice. "Even the simplest thing takes its time."

In front of Willy's he flagged a cab. Twenty minutes later Hemingway stood beside Dr. Stein's reception desk. The receptionist was cute in a plump high-school-girl way. "Can I help you?" she asked brightly. Hemingway hesitated, decided it wasn't worth the explanation, and said, "Don't worry, I'll find him myself." He walked the short corridor to the only door that was open. Inside, he found Dr. Stein sitting in an examination chair playing solitaire. When Dr. Stein looked up he did not smile.

"Should I ask what brings you here at this hour?" Dr. Stein asked.

Hemingway leaned his shoulder against the door frame. From his pants pocket he brought out a string of dental floss and began to twist it around his finger. "You know, when I got home I tried doing what you said. But I just can't seem to get the hang of it. I thought you'd give me a hand."

Dr. Stein stood slowly. "I only have the office open at this hour for emergencies. Why don't you come back tomorrow?"

"Yeah, well, you don't seem stacked with emergencies at the moment."

Dr. Stein sighed and then sat down again. "Tomorrow please, Mr. Hemingway. The mysteries of dental floss can be revealed to you then."

With the heel of his foot Hemingway kicked the door closed. Then he stepped toward Dr. Stein. From his pocket he brought out a hundred dollar bill. He waved it toward Dr. Stein. "Ever see one of these?"

Dr. Stein sighed with boredom. "From time to time but not as often as I'd like."

"Take a closer look, you might recognize this one." When Dr. Stein said nothing, Hemingway said, "Well, if you don't recognize it you should. Your wife dropped it."

"Where?" Dr. Stein said. Curiosity appeared around his eyes.

"Right into my hand. Don't you want to know why?"

Finally Dr. Stein smiled. "Am I allowed three guesses?"

"We can cut the crap any time you want," Hemingway said. When Dr. Stein said nothing more, Hemingway slowly folded the bill into a tight square.

With two fingers he slipped it into Dr. Stein's breast pocket. "See? When I find something I put it back where it belongs."

"Well!" Dr. Stein said. His smile grew wide and he leaned back in the chair. "You're the first to return the money. The others just take her money and whatever else she offers and disappear. Except for the last one; he tried to keep his part of the bargain. Things got tricky."

"I'll bet. By the way, just so you won't worry, she'll be at Chi-Chi's off Route 9 around midnight."

Dr. Stein looked hard at Hemingway. "So let's drop the other shoe; just tell me why."

After a moment Hemingway shrugged. "Guys got to look out for one another." His smile was nearly generous. "Guys got to help each other out." He stepped to where Dr. Stein sat and leaned forward. "The only friend a guy ever has is a guy."

Dr. Stein stood slowly, a look of dawning light in his eyes. Now his smile was genuine. Hemingway liked that.

"So from now on," Hemingway said as he lifted his right shoulder and drove his right fist hard into the center of Dr. Stein's face, "take better care of your friends." Dr. Stein fell to the floor in a heap, blood spattered his face.

Something snapped in Hemingway's right hand, it hurt like hell. With his left he felt it carefully. He wouldn't be able to clean his fruit-flies for a month. He hated when this happened.

He stepped to where Dr. Stein lay motionless. Hemingway bent to make sure he was still breathing and nothing was broken badly. Then he stood and left the room. On his way past the receptionist he said, "You'd better look after your boss. I think he fell down." She was already standing when he passed her, he knew the Doc would be okay.

At Philly's he bought two bottles of good bourbon and went home. His mouth was mostly under control again, but the pain-killers had all worn off and it hurt worse than ever.

Hemingway wrapped a bandage around his right hand with his left as best he could and started drinking. He had nearly dozed off when the phone finally rang. The clock read eleven-twenty. He sat up on the edge of his bed. The second time it rang Hemingway picked up the bottle and shot glass and filled one from the other. In the silence he emptied the shot glass. When the phone rang again he refilled the shot glass, in the silence he tossed it back. On the next ring he did the same, and in the silence he drank the bourbon back. He stopped counting after the sixth ring, and he fell back on his bed after several more rings, relieved when it did not ring again. He didn't remember anything after that. But it was the last time he ever went to a dentist.

EVERY YOUNG ANARCHIST

TOMORROW'S SUPPOSED to be Tuesday. So what! Time means nothing. Does God carry a watch? Does He call the Time-Lady on the telephone? Does He have a snooze alarm beside His bed set for forty lousy winks? Hell no!

So I leave calendars to the assholes who send checks; to the landlord, phone company, electric company; or greeting cards, Christmas, birthdays, Valentines, St. Patrick. Time means nothing to Barkley. When I'm hungry, I eat. Why should Barkley wait around until 'dinnertime'! What do you take me for, some kind of jerk? Think God's a jerk, too? When I get tired, I sleep. Do I stand around rubbing my eyes yawning and waiting for 'bedtime'? Know what I say? No time except the present! Am I right or what?

Example: they expect me at the bank. What the hell do I care, I've got a hundred million in that bank. So maybe I show up next week, or maybe tomorrow, or maybe in six months. What the hell; maybe I call them saying I'm never coming back, then two minutes later walk into their office demanding to know why they're all so late. What kind of rube you take me for, buddy? Let me tell you something. When I was young and stupid I carried a wristwatch. And guess what? Only thing ever happened was strangers stopped me on the street to ask the time. But Barkley got wise. Don't wear a watch and let other people track the time. Sometimes I ask twenty people in the space of ten minutes, sometimes the same person several times, sometimes for the precise second. How about that?

Listen to this: I had a job. First day, I show up at the shop at three in the morning, ready to work, work eight straight hard hours for my boss and his lousy business. What happens? I get bored waiting for him to show-up, go home, fall asleep, don't wake up until late. It was his own fault and I tell him so. He should have been there, I tell him, because Barkley was ready then, ready to work like ten men, I tell him, ready to haul ass, ready to pump iron, ready to bust balls, I tell him; I was ready.

And guess what; the guy shakes his head, tells me I'm late, says, "Shop hours are eight in the morning 'til six; regular hours for normal people." Know what I say? Bullshit! Like normal is the same as good. Just an excuse for laziness, incompetence, lack of motivation. And I tell him so. But he tells me to shut up!

Can you believe that? Says, "Be here at eight, or don't come back." Impertinence, outrage, clear symptoms of this terrible disease, Shit-for-Brains. I quit right there, on the spot. And I leave quick because I've heard Shit-for-Brains is like herpes, very contagious; you can't be too careful.

But do I give a fuck? Go ahead and ask me. I've got a hundred million in the bank. Father Time licks my asshole and thanks me for the privilege. My time is all the time there is. Time waits for nobody, except me. When I walk through the doors of that bank, all the clocks shut off. Sometimes I'm in and out in ten minutes. Sometimes I'm in there ten, twelve, even eighteen hours. Lawyers and accountants roll up their sleeves, loosen ties, drink coffee, offer me donuts; nobody thinks of going home. It isn't 'quitting time'. I call the bank manager at home, get him and his wife the hell out of bed, order him to meet me at midnight, then don't show up until four AM, leave after ten minutes. And the stupid bastard waits. I love him because he waits. Time is his incurable disease, not mine. Do I give a shit?

When I was young and still too stupid to know my ass from an ashtray, my girlfriend called me every morning at five. If I didn't answer after two rings, she'd hang up, wouldn't talk to me, insisted if I didn't answer, it could only be because I was screwing someone else. This went on; at that time I was still damn stupid.

Now I have a whole apartment building full of women, twenty-three of them, and a key to each apartment. Come and go as I please. Call one up, tell her I'm on my way, then show up at the apartment next door and make a lot of noise, just to let her know why I'm late. Sometimes I fuck three of them at once, what the hell do I care. When I come in, all of the clocks shut off, automatically, everywhere. God doesn't give a shit about time, and frankly I'm with him.

Time is for people who have diseases, take medicines, pills, tonics, injections. Sickness, rot, decay. Time is on the side of the fungus. A harvest of fungus. To hell with that. You can have that, if you want it, I won't fight you. I'll stick with my hundred million in the bank. I have ten doctors. Three of them sit beside my bed to watch me sleep. Another stays beside my toilet, measures and tests my shit each time I squat. Another takes my temperature, monitors my blood pressure whenever I watch a movie, or fuck. The other five drink coffee and worry. When I was young and stupid I got sick and suffered. Now I read about it in the newspapers.

Believe it; calendars are for assholes. Little white boxes to hide the days in. Fill them with water, paint them with blood, slash them with razors. A day is a glassful of time, gulp-gulp. A day is a fart between bowls of hot chili. A day is a load of laundry, a dope deal that falls through across town, a fuck that gets somebody pregnant. A day is a pigeon, or a ten-year old kid, smashing into your windshield and rolling off, motionless.

Little boxes to hide old masturbation fantasies, war wounds, lost double-headers, lovers who commit suicide without leaving notes. Time is a rubber crutch for the morally crippled, stumbling along an endless corridor - that ends. But fuck if I care. With a hundred million cooling in an air-conditioned vault, it's just me and God; we know what's happening. Just Him and me.

Barkley talks like a crazy man, vomits words and never wipes. His assistants carry his words away in buckets. They form a chain, a bucket brigade, while another holds a towel under his chin.

Barkley gushes the words that millions sit beside receivers waiting for. Barkley the word master, never screams, never raises his voice, even when he's especially crazy. He doesn't have to; he's a pro. But it's easy to tell when he's excited. Assistants trot nearly running, carrying silver buckets filled with writhing, slithering, wriggling words. Sometimes they slip out or spill. But there's always somebody standing by with a mop to clean up.

No question about it, Barkley is a pro. Hired the best assistants money could buy. Each could carry two buckets at a trot for one hundred yards without spilling a word. Even the guys with the mops were sharp, bobbing and weaving between running assistants, cleaning up without tripping anyone.

My first day as one of Barkley's assistants was a disaster. If I dumped one bucket I must have dumped a dozen. Finally Barkley called me over.

"I eat dumb punks like you for breakfast," he said. "Two at a time! What's your fucking problem?"

I stammered, halted, the words would not come. Barkley the pro looked at me a long, long time. "What's the matter? Shit-for-brains? You got shit-for-brains, too?" A pro through and through. Why couldn't I think of that? Why couldn't I say that? Why couldn't I just say "shit-for-brains"? Why did I just stand there with my mouth open, waiting, while Barkley could turn it off and on like a fire hydrant? After more hesitation I said, "Sorry."

Barkley looked me over with appraising, vicious eyes. "Yeah, sure. Sorry is for losers like you. Shit-for-brains, the new disease." He made me stand aside. "Learn something. Keep your eyes open and your mouth shut. You won't learn nothing with your mouth open." What a pro.

Still, he must have seen something in me, in the way I moved or something, but enough that made him keep me around. Something he could cultivate, like a good coach with a fielder who can't hit. I still made mistakes by the carload. There I was, one little bucket, trotting along beside the others carrying two large ones each. When the guys with the mops saw me coming they hovered around, waiting. Humiliating, just humiliating.

But at least I didn't suffer alone. Chuck trained with me, and he had almost as much trouble as I did. 'New meat', they called us, hooting and hollering each time either of us spilled a bucket. Misery loves company and that's the truth. Degradation, disgrace, ridicule and scorn piled on us endlessly. So he and I became friends. And really, I guess that was the point, always Barkley's purpose; even with all the mistakes we began to work as a team. Barkley was a shrewd sonofabitch, no question about it. It seemed to take forever, but finally we were carrying buckets to the end of the corridor without spilling a word.

Meanwhile, Barkley kept up the pace, kept everyone on their toes, spewing, spinning words like grace-notes, trilling then filling bucket after bucket. And as amazing as it seemed, as we got better, Barkley got better, faster, and his volume doubled, and then doubled again. More 'new meat' was hired. The drains couldn't cope, we had to build two holding tanks. Suddenly we were each made a crew leader with eight assistants; positions of responsibility, rapid advancement, climbing the ladder, it made my head spin. But really there wasn't much time to think about all of that.

Barkley kept it up, kept pouring it on, he was marvelous to watch. One man with a towel for his chin was no longer enough. Even with double shifts he was going through a towel every five minutes. Eventually we wrapped him in a plastic bib.

Only one word describes his ability, his capacity; genius. Never mind what you've heard about the others, Barkley was the only true genius. No matter how many buckets we used, he filled them all to overflowing before we could empty then. The closer he came to filling the buckets, the more urgent his flow became. Incensed by our presumption he washed us with his language. As if to insist there could never be enough buckets for him.

And, just as Barkley had the reputation for being the best, we crew-people were noticed and praised, recognized as members of a team of winners. We all sat together in the cafeteria, while assistants to the other geniuses gathered around asking what it was like up there, what was really going on, or they remained silent waiting for us to speak, to begin some bit of trivia they could take back to their co-workers as "the latest word from Barkley."

Just before the end, the Company gave each of us a parking space with our names painted on them. In a ceremony with Company officials and a photographer present we were given little plaques to take home. Just one more thing we owed to Barkley. A real pro, and we were right beside him, right up there at the top.

But nothing lasts forever, absolutely nothing. Barkley was laying it on one afternoon, driving us crazy. Three crews on 9-minute rotation, he was killing us, keeping us breathless running. And suddenly it was as though he shifted into some super- overdrive. Words poured out of him with the overwhelming silver surge of a water- cannon. Carriers all the way at the end of the corridor slipped on a floor greased with loose words, dropping whatever they were carrying, adding to the lapping at our ankles. We were covered, dripping. And the smell was horrendous. At the time it just seemed a tremendous accident. But with hind-sight I'm sure now that it was intentional. Was he trying to prove something; that even we, his hand-picked crew, weren't good enough? Of course now, no one will ever know. But even Barkley must have realized what he had done, because just as suddenly his flow diminished to nearly nothing.

We spent an entire shift cleaning up, A crew from the eighth floor offered to help, but we told them it was our mess and we'd take care of it.

But Barkley was a changed man after that. Chuck first mentioned it to me. From that day on, he seemed to become more reclusive, almost contrite, not pushing any single one of us too hard, leaving crew leaders to maintain discipline, not overworking crews wearing them out two hours before shift change.

Word of the change in Barkley got around. Workers from other crews gave us smug grins in the hallways, in the elevators. Gruff, surly, sometimes hostile scenes in the cafeteria became common. Chuck nearly came to blows with one assistant who cheerily announced that Barkley had finally lost his touch, that he couldn't cut it anymore, that in six months he'd be down to a trickle; in short, he was on his way out. When the other workers around him laughed, we agreed from then on to eat together in the lockers.

But ignoring omens never helps. It wasn't long before we began to see the signs, sure enough. Some days, in the heart of a good shift when everybody was moving, Barkley would suddenly hold back; longer than a pause, perhaps for five minutes. Everybody, the whole organization, would screech to a halt, with collisions, accidents, spillage everywhere. And then we'd wait.

Grunting and heaving, sweat pouring off his face, cheeks turning from bright red to purple to ash-grey, he'd release just on word; sort of pop it into the air and watch it spin gracefully into the bucket. No doubt about it, Barkley got tremendous satisfaction from these acrobatics, these eurhythmics.

But figures were down, the black-and-white does not lie. We let go one mop crew, and then a stand-by crew was transferred to the second floor. Believe me, Barkley was a great man, a genius no matter what they say, right up to the end. But what could we do? He began to produce small, marvelous beauties; things filled with light and graceful movement, music for the eye, for the mind. But the more beautiful, the more infrequent. Meanwhile, pressure was coming from the Office. Inspectors arrived, sometimes twice in a single shift, and Barkley took some perverse pleasure producing even less when they were watching.

With his flow cut to nearly nothing, most of us were either transferred or released. They offered me a transfer to the eighth floor, a new genius had been discovered up there, but I quit. Had to. When you've worked for the best there isn't much left. So I wasn't there, wasn't an eye-witness to the end of an era, the passing of a giant, the end of Barkley.

"The hatchet-men appeared out of nowhere," Chuck said. He and I sat behind the loading dock. I had two quarts of beer and we'd already finished the first before he could bring himself to tell the story. "You know how they are, the boys from upstairs. One minute everything is running fine, going smooth; then all of a sudden they're there, three of them, and it's like electricity, everybody stops, stands still, waiting, even though we all know what goes on from there."

"But Barkley doesn't flinch, doesn't even look up. The boys from upstairs call everybody together, order all the doors locked. You should have seen guys trying to leave, the ones who didn't want to watch, didn't want to be there for the end. Including me. But they made us all stand in a circle around Barkley. Then one of them, and I'm guessing he's the head-honcho even though they all dress alike in their neat grey suits, he starts to read the Official List of Accomplishments. And you know how with most guys that list might take ten, maybe even fifteen minutes for the guys who are really good? Well, we must have stood there close to a half-hour with this guy droning on and on."

"And there's Barkley, sitting there with his shit-eating grin, the grey-suited monkeys standing, one behind him and one to either side, and the one behind muttering through the whole thing; the whole time he's muttering, you can't make out a word, except two or three times when Barkley dozes off, falls the hell to sleep, and once even starts to snore before one of the monkeys gives him a nudge. Barkley had balls."

"Meanwhile, some of the guys are sniffling, starting to cry, you can see tears. Because everybody's thinking about the good times, the past that can never be again. When the honcho gets to the end of the list he starts about how grateful the Company is for all of the years of Barkley's hard work, and how his like will never be seen again, blah blah, blah. You could hear guys all the way in the back just breaking down, like little kids, crying."

Chuck gulped the last of the beer and heaved the bottle way out into the field behind the loading dock. Then he let out a big round belch.

"I don't know how they know it," he said. "How they signal to each other that it's over, how all three of then know to the precise second when to grab him. But they do. The two behind lunge forward, grab each of his hands and pin then back. And then slick as a snake the honcho is standing in front of Barkley with the razor already out and he slashes, bip-bop, just like that, straight across the throat, and steps aside."

"All of us, two at a time, are signaled forward. The monkeys daub each of us with some blood, the rest of the blood is carried to the drains. The honcho looks around as if to say, 'It is done,' pries open Barkley's jaws and cuts out his tongue. He holds it up for all of us to see, and then places it in a wooden box one of the monkeys is carrying. That's it. That's all. The end. What the fuck."

Chuck sits shaking his head. Myself, I knew it would happen this way, just the way he describes it. That's why I didn't want to be there. Chuck knew too, but I guess he had to see for himself. I can't blame him, not really.

"But I'll tell you what was really scary," he added. "Just as the honcho was about to slash him, this look came into Barkley's eyes. Like he was looking right at me, right into me, and through me; like he was trying to look through a fogged-over pane of glass so he could see outside, to see beyond. That no-good sonofabitch scared the fuck out of me. After all these years, that's what he leaves me with. No good sonofabitch."

Chuck's right, what else is there to say. Barkley was a crap-artist. Mister Bullshit and a stupid prick-bastard on top of that, never happier than when busting somebody's balls, watching somebody suffer. A conniving asshole posing as a genius, a con-artist of a genius. And what else can you do with a used-up, worn-out, has-been genius?

LOLLIPOP LAND

BREWSTER BEAR WAS OUT of a job again; 'made redundant' was
the euphemism applied to the former maintenance man for the Candy Cane
Apartments along Raspberry Row. As had happened before in his life, being a
bear left Brewster instantly mistrusted by the tenants. In this case the tenants
who slandered Brewster and got him fired included Dolly Duck, whose
door opened to a variety of drakes four or five times a day, and Old Mister
Alligator, who smelled bad, moved slow and spouted predation theories to
justify his continued existence. To Brewster Bear's relief and pleasure, Clarice
Chicken was one tenant he knew liked him. But the building's owner, Green-
Jelly Elephant, believing he needed Brewster's help, convinced himself that
eventually the other tenants would get used to Brewster Bear. In Lollipop
Land, this sort of thing is possible.

Life was not simple for Brewster, even at the Candy Cane apartments,
but what got him fired was his shitting in the apartment building's stairwells.
Admitting that for a bear, shitting in the woods was inevitable, Green-Jelly
Elephant insisted that Brewster Bear acknowledge that his apartment building
was not the woods, but to no good effect. So Green-Jelly Elephant regretted
the loss of such a strong employee who was also willing to work for peanuts.
But he needed to draw the line somewhere, and the Candy Cane stairwells
were not the place for a bear to relieve himself.

Stunned by his summary dismissal, Brewster Bear walked slowly along Jelly-Bean Avenue wondering how he would pay his rent. He only had a few nonpareils in his savings amount, and this week's pay had already been spent to cover the debt on his SugarCard. He circled the block several times attempting to clear his head and then returned to the Candy Cane Apartments determined to pick up his few personal possessions. And to see Clarice Chicken one last time.

When she opened her door, Brewster Bear did not step inside as he had so often before, but stood in the hallway explaining what had happened. As he spoke, Clarice Chicken pecked frantically at the threshold, her beady, black eyes sparkling with tears. After Brewster explained all that had happened, Clarice Chicken handed him fifty nonpareils, all that she had, and then gave him a peck on the cheek before closing her door. Behind the closed door she paced and clucked for a long while, until the chicks finally returned from school. She was glad to see them and relieved to be asked by them for things she knew how to do. And relieved too that this unpleasant ritual had concluded before her husband, Randi Rooster, returned from his law office.

On his walk back to his apartment, Brewster bought a copy of the Lollipop Times and when he reached his apartment he opened a can of Bubblegum juice and turned to the employment page. He needed to find a job quickly, which meant to be ready to settle for a hard job with low pay. So when he spotted a job for a shipping clerk he knew what to expect. He'd do that job as long as it had a toilet nearby.

As he had hoped, the job Brewster Bear was offered by Clyde Camel was in a shipping room that had its own toilet. Brewster Bear smiled; this was a job he could do.

And most of the time he could. Most of the objects he was asked to pack for shipping were large and sturdy and easy to manipulate. But Brewster's attempts to pack things that were small and delicate - glass, porcelain, spun sugar, even cotton candy - ended in disaster. Things cracked, things shattered, things lost parts and Brewster Bear's big bear paws just would not work. At the interview, Brewster had allowed himself to be deceived by Clyde Camel's large blue polka-dots on his bright orange fur and his broad red lips that his new employer was patient and generous. In fact, Clyde Camel was notoriously short-tempered, inclined to spit his words in angry argument. In short, he was just the opposite of what Brewster had believed. In less than a month he was once again out of a job.

Having been fired, Brewster's first thought was once again to visit Clarice Chicken. But even as this thought came to him, he recognized it was useless. She had, after all, only wanted him for his body. And he understood that even with Randi Rooster out of the way, she would have thought first of her brood and its future. What could he have offered Clarice's chicks? He was glad he passed a candystore along his way back to his apartment.

Secluded in his den Brewster reviewed the employment section of the newspaper as he began to work on a case of cheap Lemonade Made From Powder. And in his inebriated state, Brewster Bear began to curse his paws. And cursing his paws he cursed his parents and then his family. He then cursed his neighborhood and its culture which was indifferent to encouraging bears to move into the professions through extended periods of post-secondary education. Finally when he had finished off nearly half the case he resumed cursing himself. Especially he cursed the lost years along with the opportunities he had failed to recognize, more acid-bitter than those opportunities which had never been available. And finally he cursed the brilliant chances and priceless friendships which he'd tossed aside like sheets of used toilet paper. With caustic tears of self-pity squeezed from the cheap lemonade clouding his sight, Brewster stood to relieve himself of grief and shame. Brewster finally agreed that he needed to find a job where his big bear paws could do simple things. With only a few cans of Lemonade left and nearly at the bottom of the classifieds, an ad for drivers for Lemon Drop Cab Company caught his attention. It seemed to him that perhaps his perfect job was to drive a cab. This idea came as a revelation; as if it had always been there behind his eyes waiting to be seen. That night Brewster Bear slept soundly, experiencing for the first time the sensation of seeing his destiny as a long straight ribbon of licorice unrolling shiny black to the horizon.

Early the following morning Brewster arrived at the door to the Lemon Drop Cab Company and he fell in love instantly with the bright yellow uniforms the cab drivers wore along with the bright yellow cabs they drove. After the interview, his new supervisor, Arty Aardvark, led him to the parking lot and suggested he get behind the wheel of a cab. Standing beside one, Brewster Bear was startled by how small its door was. But with a little effort he got snugly in.

To his delight Brewster discovered that his big bear paws were no problem operating the steering wheel or the gear shift or even the emergency break. But to his horror he discovered that his big bear foot hit the gas and the break pedals at the same time. He drove into three parked cabs before he even left the lot, and he became so confused at the driveway that mistakenly he turned into oncoming traffic. So he did not see the ice cream truck until it was too late. The driver of the ice cream truck, Harry Hedgehog, flew through his windshield and landed on Brewster's cab's hood, and then he did not move. Brewster Bear was frozen with horror. Without realizing it, he relieved himself copiously in the driver's seat of the cab.

Eventually the Lollipop Cops arrived. When they finished chasing witnesses and bystanders with bottles of seltzer, one Cop pushed his large red nose and fuzzy red-haired head into the driver's window and firmly told Brewster Bear to shut off the engine and step slowly out of the cab. Brewster Bear did just what the Lollipop Cop told him to do. The Lollipop Cops sprayed Brewster Bear with seltzer and put him in licorice handcuffs before tossing him into the back of the Jelly-Bean Jail Wagon. Brewster was driven away to the sound of loud cat-sirens. Harry Hedgehog, father of five and recently separated from Dorothy Hedgehog, died the following morning at Gingerbread Memorial Hospital.

Brewster did not enjoy his night on the hard plank bed in the Pretzel-Stix Holding Cell, but he relieved himself in utter terror the next morning when he was introduced to his attorney, Randi Rooster. After a brief, respectful peck of greeting, Randi Rooster broke the news of Harry Hedgehog's death, and told him that the State's Prosecutor, Larry Lizard, would indict him for second-degree murder. Randi Rooster did not smile when he explained to Brewster that, considering his blood-sugar levels and the condition of his paws, the State had a strong case.

Brewster Bear was speechless and hoped Randi Rooster mistook his astonishment for concern over the case against him. He had never asked, and Clarice Chicken had never told him, if Randi Rooster knew about their affair. He searched his attorney's narrow face for any sign. But after a moment he decided none of this mattered; in Zoo- Prison they have no toilets, and he trembled at the thought of being some gorilla's best friend. Randi Rooster then asked him to describe exactly what happened. And Brewster did.

Randi Rooster studied him as Brewster spoke, and Brewster felt every second of his scrutiny as it dripped by. Finally Randi Rooster explained that the Lemon Drop Cab Company was also being held responsible, and that Arty Aardvark swore he had refused Brewster the job because he was clearly drunk, but Brewster had insisted he needed the job, had grabbed the keys out of Arty's hand and then had driven off before he could be stopped. Randi Rooster paused before asking Brewster if there was any truth to it.

Even as Brewster Bear growled and snarled his denial, he wondered if Randi Rooster, bent on revenge, was setting him up for a long stretch behind chicken wire. It all came down to whether or not he knew of the affair. Randi Rooster appeared to listen intently while he pecked and clucked at the top of the conference table, but the hard look of his tiny black eyes told Brewster nothing.

Brewster Bear was arraigned that afternoon. At the hearing Brewster Bear was intimidated. The Hedgehog family was in attendance, the tearful widow snarling and spitting in his direction. Larry Lizard was a brash young iguana prosecuting attorney for the City, quick and precise in his movements. He began his argument with the insistence that Brewster be given the maximum sentence. But the hearing had hardly begun when Randi Rooster loudly motioned to challenge the State's most powerful piece of evidence, insisting that the blood-sugar samples had been tainted and contaminated by the usual Lollipop Cops ineptitude since there had been red hair and seltzer residue in all of them. Hearing this, Judge Owen Owl fluttered his wings and angrily remarked on the tragic implications of clownish incompetence and then reminded the Chief of the Lollipop Cops Department, Rolly Dodger, that his budget had been increased each year, but buffoonery still reigned within the department. With a single whack of his enormous gavel, Judge Owen Owl declared Brewster Bear innocent for lack of evidence, and reminded the Chief of Police and the City's Prosecutor that he would nail both of their skulls to the floor if they came to his courtroom again with such a shoddy case. Then as was his duty, Rolly Dodger cleared the courtroom, chasing everyone to the exits by squirting them copiously with bottled seltzer.

When they had dried out, Randi Rooster took Brewster Bear to the Grape Soda Lounge, just two blocks away. They took a booth in the back, Brewster could just fit in. As this was a well-known watering hole for all of City Hall, he could hardly keep from turning his head recognizing one powerful character after another.

Root beers, candy cigarettes and truffles finally reached the table. Randi Rooster seemed to relax and asked Brewster what he planned to do now. Brewster wanted to put the best face on his future assuring him he expected something to turn up any day now.

Randi Rooster offered sympathy and then suggested he had a client who
might offer Brewster some work. When asked if he'd be willing to meet
with him Brewster Bear agreed. Randi Rooster's shiny black eyes remained
emotionless as he passed a slip of paper to him with an address on it written in
chicken scratch. Then Randi Rooster told him he had another appointment,
hopped off his perch and wished Brewster good luck. He was already gone
when Brewster Bear realized that for the first time since the accident he
was smiling. Brewster relieved himself out of relief, and he concluded that
fortunately, Randi Rooster could never have known. When finally he lumbered
out of the Grape Soda Lounge a bit tipsy from the powerful root-beer, he
realized his smile was broad but also firm, a smile that would endure. Things
would get better when he had a job.

The address Randi Rooster gave Brewster Bear was a very exclusive apartment
building in a secluded neighborhood off Cotton Candy Court. When the
apartment door opened Brewster was startled to recognize Humphrey Maltese
Falcon, a wealthy and well-respected entrepreneur. Falcon looked him up and
down before inviting him inside. Brewster followed him to the sunken living-
room. Falcon offered him a root-beer while he explained that Randi Rooster had
told him all about Brewster's problem. With a wing propped against the fireplace
he explained to Brewster that he regarded his clients as his friends, and so he has
always been happy to help them out with loans at very modest terms of repayment.
And that to his relief and delight, he had found that the majority of his clients were
honest, and that very few actively evaded repayment. With a sigh and a flutter he
admitted that for those few occasions when the most energetic cajolery did not
seem to work, unfortunately only very strong measures would set the books even.
Falcon flew to a perch on the edge of the couch beside Brewster.

In a conspiratorial whisper, he promised to pay Brewster well if he would
simply visit those few reluctant clients and remind them of their obligation.
Falcon insisted there should be no rough stuff since he was not interested in
paying for broken parts. He then expressed admiration at the breadth and
power of Brewster Bear's paws and insisted with awe that the mere sight of
them was to recognize their destructive power. He was confident the sight of
those paws would send nonpareils flowing from the driest of wells. Brewster
looked at his paws. Even as a cub he had found them awkward and obnoxious
and embarrassing. But as he held them up and turned them, he recognized that
they really were magnificent. And he understood how a guilt-ridden conscience

might become intimidated in their presence. But also that finally he had found a job they could do, and perhaps something that only they could do well.

And so events worked out, to Brewster Bear's great relief. All that this new job demanded he do was look menacing when the client opened the doors, and suddenly that reluctant client was finding nonpareils everywhere. Brewster Bear had never even had to raise his paw. Soon, his employment had brought Falcon enough nonpareils to allow Brewster to move into one of the new high-rise caves. Everyone was happy with his efforts, especially Humphrey M. Falcon. So happy in fact that one evening he invited Brewster Bear to a private dinner at his apartment. But when he arrived, Brewster Bear was startled to discover that their dinner companions consisted of Randi Rooster and Clarice Chicken.

Brewster sat across from Randi Rooster, while to his right sat Humphrey M. Falcon, and on Randi's left sat Clarice Chicken. Though Brewster resisted the thought, he wondered again if Randi Rooster had known. Except that now, he wondered if Falcon had also known. Brewster sniffed the air for conspiracy. But Clarice Chicken looked lovelier than ever.

Brewster restrained himself throughout dinner, paws out of sight unless demanded, engaging only in quiet conversation. At one point Randi Rooster turned and congratulated Brewster on his exceptional success as Falcon's aide. With a smirk Randi told Clarice Chicken that the emergency wards were filling up with Mr. Falcon's impertinent clients. Brewster restrained his rage at this slander. After all, he was proud that he had never hurt anyone while collecting Falcon's debts. But then, almost as a gesture of concession, Randi Rooster added that he had never believed that Brewster had been guilty in the death of Harry Hedgehog. Falcon wondered aloud if Randi Rooster hadn't had his eye out on his behalf for such talent for some time. Then Falcon told him he valued the introduction to Brewster so much that he had gladly canceled that inconvenient but timely loan Randi Rooster had taken out against Clarice Chicken's insurance policy, and assured him that the policy was once again fully in effect. Brewster felt the fur at the back of his neck lightly stiffen. With nodding embarrassment Randi Rooster complained of being over-worked, and grinned at Clarice Chicken before conceding how useful it would be to have such an assistant as Brewster. Then he asked Clarice Chicken if she thought such an assistant might be useful around the house.

Icy water suddenly passed through Brewster's veins; Randi Rooster knew, probably had known all along. Why hadn't Clarice Chicken warned him?

Randi then burst into loud laughter clucking and pecking at the table top, as if he had merely described an outrageous fantasy. Brewster glanced at Falcon to discover how far the secret had traveled but learned nothing. Meanwhile, Clarice Chicken clucked and pecked with slow methodical strokes, as if each gesture represented a separate thought. Just then, Paulie Penguin, Falcon's butler and chef, appeared to announce that desert and liquors would be served in the Library. All Brewster wanted to do was go home. How could he have let himself fall into this?

The four stood and made their way toward the Library. Clarice Chicken turned to say she would powder her beak. After a moment Randi Rooster volunteered to follow her so that she did not become lost in the grand apartment. Brewster and Falcon took seats in the Library. Brewster Bear yearned for relief, but managed to contain himself with the anticipation of being with Clarice Chicken again, even under these circumstances.

Brewster Bear and Humphrey M. Falcon had just taken seats across from each other when they heard loud squawking coming from the hallway. Instinctively Brewster stood to see what the problem was. Unhappily for everyone, he came upon Randi Rooster and Clarice Chicken in an argument that was about to become violent. Without thinking, Brewster stepped in front of Clarice Chicken. But in doing this Randi Rooster assumed Brewster was about to attack him, and leapt, claws ripping the air, in Brewster's direction. At that moment, Clarice Chicken stepped from behind Brewster Bear toward safer shelter, and Randi Rooster's right fore-claw sank into her left eye, then slipped past her beak to become lodged in her jugular vein. She dropped to the ground dead. Stunned by his own fury, Brewster's paw flew instinctively, caught Randi Rooster in midair as if he was a salmon, flung him against the far wall and hard enough to kill him.

Even as Clarice Chicken sank to the floor, Falcon realized his friend Randi Rooster was in deep trouble, and flew at Brewster Bear's face with claws forward and bared. But Brewster flung him away with the follow-through of his blow to Randi and without even turning his head. Within three seconds, three fowl friends lay dead at Brewster Bear's feet.

Brewster lifted Clarice Chicken carefully into his ample lap, and stroked the feathers of her head while tears fell in large drops from his eyes. After a few moments of silence, Paulie Penguin emerged cautiously from the kitchen. His beak fell open as he surveyed the carnage, but when he realized that Brewster

was now looking directly at him, he scuttled away. In moments Brewster Bear
could hear him squawking frantically into the telephone for the Lollipop Cops.

The Cops found him exactly where he had been, Clarice Chicken's body still
cuddled in his lap, big round tears still falling from his eyes. The Lollipop Cops
spent ten minutes chasing each other with oversize hammers and spraying each
other from large glass bottles of seltzer, until finally the Coroner, Dr. Raymond
Crocodile, made his appearance.

At the trial, Dr. Raymond Crocodile asserted that all of the wounds were
consistent with a sudden and powerful attack from a large clawed creature,
and Paulie Penguin insisted that Humphrey M. Falcon had expressed deep
concern about how the dinner would turn out. Brewster Bear's attorney in this
trial was Dewey Duck of the law firm Dewey, Chittem and Howe. He had
volunteered to handle his case for free if Brewster signed over all negotiable
rights to his story. As always, Brewster Bear did as he was asked. Unfortunately
for him, a certain inclination to spit as he spoke reduced Dewey's effectiveness
on Brewster's behalf, and left the jury wet but unimpressed. But even this was of
no consequence. Larry Lizard got just enough Clowns on the jury to guarantee
Brewster's case was hopeless. With Judge Owen Owl's approval, Larry Lizard
paraded a string of Falcon's clients to the witness stand swearing, one after
the other, that Brewster had beaten them senseless and then threatened their
wives and children, all to exhort thousands of nonpareils from them. Brewster
assumed the accusation would be treated as a joke and waited for someone
to stand and confess the charade. Judge Owen Owl shook his head often
during the testimony, and blinked with transcendent concentration. But the
conclusion could not have been clearer; Judge Owen Owl announced that Life
Was A Jungle, and The Law of the Jungle would prevail. Brewster felt more
astonishment than fear, as if he was on the set of the wrong movie, and simply
waited until someone noticed and pointed him in the right direction.

Though brutal, the justice of the Courts was swift, and in the end Brewster
Bear sat in his cage only regretting that he did not have more to regret.
Opportunities for regret had come rarely in Brewster Bear's life as they do for
most bears. If only he'd had more to regret, he might find this moment nearly
reassuring and it would be easier to resign himself to this ultimate injustice.
But as the hours to his execution ticked down, he found himself more and
more lost in the happy memories of carefree days of cub-hood, of charging
across meadows in bright, sweet spring with light like golden honey all around

him and in his nose and in his heart, so that he had felt he could run nearly into the sky; his heart had seemed so light and free he needed to concentrate in order to not float away. From time to time memories of Clarice Chicken came to mind as well. And gradually he understood that she had simply been one more escape for him, one more opportunity to leave the bounds of his ungainly body, and to touch the face of Perfect Beauty.

Brewster juggled these and other thoughts, so that though he had not intended it, as his day approached he found himself finally and utterly resigned. All of the Zoo Keepers remarked how calm Brewster appeared that last day; his demeanor leading them to wonder if this execution was actually too nice. But this window of wonderment closed quickly; Brewster Bear was executed for the deaths of Randi Rooster, Humphrey Maltese Falcon, and Clarice Chicken by the lethal injection of unfiltered glucose at precisely 6 AM, and was declared officially expired at 6:18 AM.

Green-Jelly Elephant read of the execution in the morning's newspaper and became so depressed he decided to take the rest of the day off. Though there was no way for him to be certain, he believed that in the end Brewster Bear had forgiven every one for all that had happened to him, even himself.

Because in Lollipop Land, this sort of thing is possible.

SALLY & THE DISASTERS:
SCENES FROM A MUSICAL LIFE

1.

In this version, Sally plays the vibraphone in the Disasters band. The vibraphone resembles a xylophone so much that there's no point to further comment. She also writes most of the music the band performs, but only in this version. Sally has discovered that Reality is that which is endured.

"This is the piece I was telling you about," Sally says. "I've circled all the hard parts in red so we can practice them hard. I have written the hardest parts I can so that we will achieve bar-line nirvana, with intensive disorientation, after only four and a half hours of continuous practice."

In his suavest Utter asks, "Sweetheart, just what country are you from?" Utter is the tallest member of a short band.

"One of the really big ones," she says, a dismissive sneer veils her distress. "Probably the biggest. Or if not the biggest, maybe the second or third biggest. But it's right up there." The serenity of her smile kicks Utter in the shin and he hobbles to a corner more bemused than distressed.

Complete says to Nuclear, "I told you! Did I tell you or what? Can I pick an accent or what?" Complete and Nuclear trade quips often, which annoys Sally to distraction, but bonds them in a useful way.

Sally recognizes an approaching band-mutiny as a form of musical bad weather that might result in interesting work. "Accent? I speak an uninflected version of American, indistinguishable from the melodious tones of your central Californian. This is the language as spoken by your community's most visible members."

"Members, ugh, ugh," Utter says. "She said visible members."

"What Utter's trying to say," Complete says, "is that your way of speaking is getting in the way of what you want to say. So to speak." He then begins a series of violent gymnastic activities meant to increase heart-rate and blood pressure to the point where he loses consciousness. Intending to scare the shit out of everybody and thereby leave him alone, it also allows him, once he regains consciousness, to learn the musically perverse parts Sally writes. Complete has been with the band the longest; he has been here before.

"There he goes!" cries Nuclear. "Will nothing stop him?"

"The planes can't stop him," Utter chants as a monk sings Gregorian, "the trains can't stop," Nuclear harmonizes a two-part invention, "the army can't stop him, his mother can't stop him." Pause. "Will this be the end?" All genuflect. Utter is the newest member of the band and exudes a deepening sense of regret.

"I'll stop him," Arthur announces bravely and dives to the floor beneath the whirling Complete. To no good end. Arthur is neither the tallest nor the oldest nor the newest band member, and he rarely quips. Thus, he is the band member least likely to get paid or laid.

Later, during a particularly difficult passage, Complete turns to Nuclear muttering, "I would derive a great deal more satisfaction from these musical sculptures if you were stoned."

"Same here," Nuclear mutters bluntly in return. When Complete runs out of band members to mutter at he mutters to Nuclear.

Nirvana is achieved as Complete finishes playing the hardest part on the score; a soliloquy for trash can and rolled paper-towels. Arthur, who has just managed a furious run of triplets on the telephone receiver, gasps, "Can I at least get paid now?" The silence that follows is not profound.

2.

Arthur is no longer speaking. In this version he has suffered a disequilibrium.

And it is the startlement, the surprise at being surprised, of his discovery that he precipitates himself fitfully into this corner, at this moment, temporarily safe from his daemon, his temptress, Rita, his musical instrument.

His is a bitter epiphany. He has come to recognize the futility of his ax, the musiconophone. He has discovered that the ultimate barrier has been reached. Having reached an unsurpassable point, an apex, his instrument has begun to destroy him. In his musical experimental laboratory, Arthur has become overwhelmed by the fearful arrogance of his creations, those large, lumpy things slowly coming to life under his fingers. And Rita, his dear and precious musiconophone, reclines alluringly in crushed wine-red velvet, lips slightly parted.

Sally opens another can of beer impressed when she does not get any on her t-shirt.

Turning a single sheet of score paper dense with small black notes around and around still looking for the beginning, Complete announces, "This is not what they taught us in counterpoint class."

Arthur trembles in a corner mute and tormented. He reminds Utter of Lon Chaney Jr. in THE WEREWOLF when he's being taken over by the werewolf thing but he's fighting against it for the sake of the girl.

Absolute squats beside Arthur, his nine-sting guitar set to an obscure Chinese tuning and plucks sharply. "It is this dreadful arrogance," Arthur says huskily in a tv German accent. "As if to say I know something more, something better, something more beautiful than Schoenberg or Ives or my cousin Roscoe. The French say that arrogance is a form of contempt." Absolute plucks furiously in accompaniment to Arthur's words until a string snaps slashing his cheek. When Absolute finishes and puts the guitar aside, he tries to use his copy of the score to roll a joint, but the shit keeps falling out the ends. Glancing over, Arthur comments, "Nada por nada, if you catch my meaning."

Sally puts her wet beer can on her copy of the score. "Roscoe's a pretty hip guy, Arthur. Do you really think he's got something we can use?" She smiles, amazed to watch the ink run, nice patterns. "Something with like sort of nice patterns."

"Man, if I get a whiff of any more nice patterns, I'll have an up-chuck that will gross out the mob. I ain't fooling." Nuclear has taken responsibility for playing all the percussion parts because he hopes to fuck up and get thrown out of the band so he can join Johnny and the Rocket Assholes, which has played twice in the last month and everybody in that band is getting laid.

"Listen, man," Sally says calmly, "we're not throwing you out of the band, and that's that." Her beer is avoiding her mouth by running over her chin as part of an exercise in self-denial. "And that Johnny and his Rocket Assholes is a sucky band, anyway."

"And the guy's name isn't even Johnny." Utter wonders if he can slip out because there's this girl. "I'm going for cigarettes; does anybody want anything?"

Sally drains her beer having broken several solemn vows with one flick of her mind, and then smashes the empty can under the heel of her right boot. "Now listen here, I've got a hot date with a chiropractor who thinks cocaine is the drug of love; so if we could finish this off quick I'd really appreciate it."

Absolute stands and walks over to her, nearly slips on the wet and flattened aluminum. "Will you kindly restrain your outrage. Arthur is suffering a major artistic crisis. How can you make glib comments from a medical point of view? And while I'm thinking about it, you tell that little suckass you been porking to keep his hot pudgy fingers out of my stash."

Nuclear steps forward. "Our musical self-importance is not at issue here, even less the selfishness of our physical appetites. Arthur's crisis is our crisis. He's in the band."

"Well," Sally says, "this band's just one step away from truck-stop music, and I'll bail like nobody's business before we get there." Her chiropractor of bright colors has promised to leave his wife just as soon as the kids graduate from college. Sally has done the math and is thoroughly relieved. "Besides, you only get so many nights of ecstasy."

"And I suppose," Nuclear speculates dubiously, "there are higher gratifications than the melodious and propulsive tremor, the acoustic thrill of Arthur's bewailing musiconophone solos." Nuclear cannot understand why he hasn't been thrown out of this band yet. If it was up to him, he'd have thrown himself out long ago. But he keeps thinking he's trying.

"Arthur has gotten himself into this," Sally sneers. "All he needs to do is take Rita back. So she spent some time somewhere else. And maybe somebody's hands got on her and thrilled her deliciously. And maybe she even liked it. But if he thinks so much about the music he makes, let him prove it. Otherwise maybe we all should start packing."

"I'll do it!" Arthur leaps to the instrument's carrying case snatching up Rita as he goes, stops to stand beside the window in the full light of day, takes Rita into his hands and fingers every aperture he has been trained to caress. Nuclear misses the introduction, but his mistake is so perfect that Arthur smiles.

Utter leaves his stand of percussionist paraphernalia, unsurprised that no one notices his absence, but delighted there are so many nice patterns.

3.

This version deals primarily with a problem involving musical interpretation, but secondarily with trash bags and the class struggle.

Initially, trash bags are deployed in the fourth floor rehearsal apartment laid-out like a shotgun shack according to astrological parameters. Thus, wet garbage bags in the first room where no one would sleep on a dare, in the second newspapers are piled (this is Complete's bedroom-cum-garden) with pot plants in the closet for the right touch of nature. In the next, empty plastic spring-water bottles are strung on a rope from the ceiling encircling (this is Utter's bedroom- cum-ranch) that cockroach village inside his mattress for the right touch of nature. Sally's room which is furthest back has never been seen, except by certain celebrities and only after the bars have closed.

These arrangements are changed with a lunar regularity. The next full moon is approaching and Sally contemplates possible changes as she sits in the corner of the front rehearsal room and closest to the window. Wistfully she says, "This, all of this, is messing up my music." She gazes across the air shaft to a brick wall and further plans her misspent youth.

"What action, Jackson?" Presley is here today. Sally usually never allows him around except after the bars close and before the sun's up.

"Fuck off, Presley." Complete sprawls in a chair beside the gutted Steinway upright piano now filled with six hundred blinking Christmas lights. Staring at it is making him pleasantly dizzy. He does not look directly at Presley, in fact he is not sure he has ever actually seen him.

Presley says, "Swing, baby, swing," and scratches his crotch.

"Resonances have begun to elude me." Sally taps the side of her head. "It's the olfactory factor. My olfactory nerves are over-active due to a certain atmosphere. It's blocking the aural inputs, the line is overloaded, how can the machine ever rest?"

"She can't hear shit 'cause she's smelling it." Utter nods transfixed with astonishment.

Reginald, friend of Presley and generally so invisible he is run over regularly by small cars, says, "It could happen."

"Did you hear something?" Sally taps the side of her head again.

"Are we getting this on video tape?" Nuclear calls out from his bedroom-cum-studio.

Snarling and dyspeptic, "This is something to get on video. We could do something with this. Maybe use it for our next album."

Utter mutters, "How could our first album be our next album?" Happily for everyone his question falls on deaf ears.

"I knew a guy," Reginald says.

Presley says, "Shake it, don't break it."

"There it goes again," Sally mutters. "I know I hear that."

Complete stands up. "Get the camera." But already Nuclear is armed, the lens falling straight through to Sally's olfactory apparatus. "Hey sweetheart, put on an earring for the close-up." Complete paces behind Nuclear who now holds the camera at his hip.

"I'm getting this shadow." Nuclear stares into the viewer, turns his hips to aim the camera and also see the monitor. "How much you want to bet Reginald is around somewhere."

"The resonances are fading, I'm hearing in black-and-white." Sally resumes her air of distracted despondency.

"What a concept!" Reginald spins turning around in the spot he is standing in, generally the only way people can see him. Or so he has decided. He makes the one friend he has dizzy. "That concept is making me dizzy; it is such a concept."

"I told you he was here, goddamit!" Nuclear is more grumpy than furious. "Who let that no-talent piss-ass in here? He's going to ruin everything he can't steal." Nuclear is consistantly concerned about the theft of his art and has considered making his concern for his art his new art. "And you know how I hate that."

"How much you want to bet Presley's still here, too." Complete sits down in the center of the room and folds his legs. "What we need now is the appropriate music. Something that will fold time and space and put zero's in my bank account."

"Arthur will be here any moment." Reginald is now lying on his back immediately in front to the door.

"What time is it?" Sally taps her wrist where no wristwatch is enwrapped. Then she taps the side of her head.

"Chantilly lace." Presley is now shaking all over.

"Wait, I'm hearing something." Sally has stood and begun to pace.

"The moon is nearly full," Utter announces as he looks out the window and sees the brick-wall air shaft. "Something is happening."

"Yes, now that you mention it," Complete says with some surprise. "I am beginning to feel the pull." He paces more slowly, apparently disturbed by the changes he feels immanent in his immediate environment. "Perhaps it is time."

"I can feel Arthur's approach like a natural phenomenon." Total has just awakened. He stumbles into the room from his room which is just a room with several piles of pornographic magazines located strategically at those corners sufficient to maintain the balance of a room whose balance is in constant peril and needs constant attention.

"It's the moon," Utter announces.

"I'm going to have to agree with you there." Complete stops pacing. "It's true what they say."

"And just what do they say?" Arthur asks. He steps through the reclining Reginald without comment, an exercise filled with mystery and transcendence. He has decided to chart the band's evolving astrological environment.

"Nature will not be denied." Complete has come to his feet in acknowledgment of Arthur's arrival and his decision.

"She's my little duce coupe." Presley smiles.

"I know I heard something then." Sally begins to pace back and forth where Complete has left off. It is something she has seen other musicians do musically and occasionally to their advantage.

"When I have finished charting our future, we will begin." Arthur takes Sally into his arms.

She breaks away with a pirouette and yells, "I wish all you fucking guys would clear the fuck out of here and clean up all this fucking trash or take it with you so I can get some goddam work done, motherfuckers. That's what I fucking wish, all right."

"The moon." Utter stares at the brick wall air shaft. "Everything is following the plan." He smiles with a pleasurable relief.

4.

"There's a fundamental point that needs to be made right here and now." In this version, Arthur is sprawled on the broken couch between the two windows against the wall of the rehearsing apartment/studio, status dependent on whichever is happening, and only as long as no one is asleep there or balling; then the space is called something else.

Utter is slouched in a chair on the verge of changing the space from a rehearsal room to a place to sleep - bedroom, perhaps. The threat is real, but the outcome remains in doubt. He wonders if his chair is far enough from Arthur. "This kind of talk," he says, "is always so one-dimensional, always so categorical without reference to ontology or geology or anything else for smart people. These are the things that make one- dimensional talk so annoying, and let's face it, so one-dimensional."

Undistracted, Nuclear goes into the kitchen, wherefrom a noise of clatter etc. is heard. "Arthur, did you go out for that beer or what?"

"But that is the fundamental point." Arthur slides from the broken couch to the floor gracefully, stretches out his full though diminutive length. "Can it be said that, for example, beer has been gotten?" From floor-level Arthur's voice is hard to distinguish. Also, he has turned his face so that it now faces the side of the couch, thus reducing the chance that he will be either seen or heard. And he can't remember what he did with the beer money.

"Anybody care to indulge a speculation about what we're going to play for that Panamanian tap-dancer?" Complete enters through the front door, Shithead, the macaw, is perched on his forearm. "The gig's tonight and we haven't rehearsed once." Shithead shits on Complete's forearm, it drips green and white with loud plops to the floor, very audible. Startled, Complete shakes the bird from his arm, it flies to its perch at the other end of the room. The shit, however, remains. "The point needs to be made that we have already gotten paid, and Arthur carries the money."

"The only distinction between an untruth and a lie is in the heart and hand of the power insuring those distinctions." Arthur's face is nearly buried behind the cushions beside the couch.

Sally is still asleep in her room, a hang-over has been surmised, and Utter notes the possibility she may not awake until after these questions, and others, have been answered.

"What's the scoop, Arty-boy?" The front door opens with a bang that startles Shithead from his perch, sending him careening and screeching, a cloud of loud, vicious green feathers, around the room, trapped. In his long black leather coat, Howard walks slowly into the room, smirking from behind instant-zap mirror shades.

"Jesus Christ, Howard," Complete bellows from a standing position, "where the fuck you been?" Complete's hair is enraged, he struggles to control a synchronized movement of arms and shoulders and hands, concerned that someone might get hurt. The effort of standing becomes tedious after a few moments. Complete sits down already figuring how much the bastard owes him. The bastard.

The door to Sally's bedroom flies open, she leaps into the rehearsal room barely clutching her robe, eyes glowing likes bowls of hash. To Howard she screeches, "The last job you got us was over two months ago, you little scumbag." Fists enraged she charges at Howard. "And now that we got this tap-dancer job ourselves and we get paid, now you're sniffing around. I've got you, you shit, you no good shit. We fired you three weeks ago so clear out of here or I'll cut your scabby balls off. We fired you!" Head shaking hair flying stomping her feet, Sally looks for all the world like she might burst asunder.

Howard rocks on his heels and he smirks and he smirks.

"And don't come back," she continues, "until you find us another goddamn job!" She turns so quickly her robe flares up to her naked waist. In a flash she's back in her room, the door crashes shut.

"Tisk, tisk, tisk," Howard says. He sucks his front tooth as he turns to Utter who is still lying on the floor and now with his eyes closed. Howard lowers his shades in one suave move. "A bit testy, don't you think? Perhaps something specifically female?"

"This is it, Howard." Utter slowly stands, then realizes he can't exactly remember why. "Isn't there something you wish to tell us, Howard? It's okay, you can open up. We're your friends."

"It's nice to see," Howard muses with a bright white grin, "a certain independence of spirit in the band again. Perhaps this will be reflected in your up-coming but, alas, perhaps last performance. That would most certainly be a shame. And a great loss to music and its public, no doubt. However, might I remind you to be a bit less rude to the person who in fact and by signed contract still owns all of your fucking instruments."

"Hey, wait a minute." Complete begins to tremble with rage. He pauses to note that he enjoys the adrenalin rush. "We paid for two of the cymbal stands, one of the mics, and all of the mic stands and cables. And we paid for one of the bass columns." Complete grabs a piece of paper and pencil, scribbles frantically on his knee a series of numbers of mystical dimension, having merely to do with the mythology of cash. "And not only that, but since you haven't paid us for that gig in April and two more in June, I figure the money we owe you and the money you owe us cancels out even."

Howard's smirk explodes into a grin. "But how can that be if you have not paid me for last night?"

Arthur has snaked his body slowly under the couch, with one small shrug he disappears completely, now working his way to the back and then along the wall, snaking his way half-slithering. Is this me, he wonders, is this what I have become? Have I come here to go this way at this moment for this reason? What would Kahlil Gibran say? Be what you are as you are and only as you are. Be what you must when you must be. You are part of all this shit, though this be really fucked. Eventually Arthur reaches the door, look at those assholes, fuck you.

Utter grinning wryly, the only grin he has, has watched Arthur while thinking there is only luck and the devil and no space in-between.

5.

In this version, Sally sings lead to the Disasters band. Sally says, "We have a job next Friday at the Fort Washington Motor Lodge."

Nuclear says, "Another job we don't get paid."

Sally says, "We're not getting paid now. So we'll play in front of an audience. What's the difference where you play if you're not getting paid."

Complete says, "If we're not going to get paid, why move the equipment and gas the truck and drive the hell out there?"

"We've been over all this before," Sally says. "If you don't play for free, you'll never get paid."

Multiple says, "Expenses sure are high." Multiple is still a band member in this version.

"What expenses?" Sally asks. "When was the last time you paid rent? And you never eat here so where's the money for food? What else? Rolling papers? Guitar strings?"

"I play the drums," Multiple says, looking stung.

"Sorry. Sticks, wood; really."

"Now hold on," Complete says standing by the open window. Weather, he notices, is getting in all over the place. "Multiple's got a point. But never mind that, just tell me what's in it for you."

"People," Sally says with surprise. "People other than you. People who never heard of me when they come in, but they'll wonder where I've been when they leave. Those people."

"So, it's like a personal thing with you," Multiple says. "For, I mean, like, the band and everything. For when we get good and stuff. I hear you."

"Give me a break." Nuclear handles the joint with studied elegance. "If we ever get around to getting good I want to be the first to hear it."

"You got that right." Utter speaks in definitive accents. "And we play any more of these free gigs I'll go goddam broke." He flexes his arm and trembles in grey, wet air.

"Why's it every time we play for free I lose money?"

"'Cause free ain't cheap enough," Nuclear says to Utter.

"What you fail to understand is how successful we are," Sally says.

Utter and Nuclear look at each other, nodding faces, nodding heads.

"Not me," Complete says from the open window. Weather is now up to his waist.

"Success? I walk into a club and see all those empty seats, see those waitresses sitting around playing pinochle with the bus boys, I say to myself, 'this is it'. Nobody has to tell me we're at the very top of our profession. So to speak."

Arthur says, "It is these songs, the songs I write." Arthur writes the songs in this version, songs which Sally must sing despite her acres of chagrin. "The songs I write make people so happy they leave. My songs make people so sad they leave. These songs make people so thoughtful, they must think. My songs just are there, like that, so to speak, without regard, sort of regardless. You know."

"These songs," Complete says as he turns to the weather-filled window, all that weather out there and no room to be. So he thinks about these songs. Just as Utter is thinking about all these mother-fucking songs; music so opaque you stick your head in them you could drown. Songs that drip from your ears afterwards. Songs of worlds that music could make.

Multiple says, "So what the fuck there, Arty-boy, what have you got up your demented sleeves there? More songs no doubt. Bugger me and call me cutie I'll have to learn the weirdest little drum figures like to make a monkey go blind. If you don't mind me saying, I think I'll just go and get myself fucked up instead of waiting for you to do it for me."

Nuclear is looking at Sally now in a way that makes Sally apprehensive without being fearful although somewhat paranoid, what with all the paranoia going around who notices the extra bits, though still not hostile either, although somewhat more combative than usual, well, why not, with the all that's everywhere so you can't turn a corner without seeing more of it.

"I believe," Arthur says while lying on his back on the floor with his eyes closed, "a situation is set for us at the Fort Washington Motor Lodge." Sally and the rest of the Disasters come to squat, crouch, sit, kneel and stand around him, as they feel at the moment most comfortable while maintaining a sufficient decorum given the situation, circumstance and company. "The situation is there, and we are here. I have just written nine new songs, none of which the band can learn in less than a week, and the gig is Thursday. Suppose we begin."

It takes hours of cigarette smoke, and gallons of beer and any amount of farting and piles of musty socks, along with the latest in pharmacological advantages, until all the weather is cleaned out of the apartment, and the band can finally get down to practice.

Perhaps, Sally muses prophetically between stanzas, there is life after music. Nuclear appraises her grinning. Sally feels herself suddenly flush with the despair of hope.

AT THE GATES OF THE MUSEUM

1

AT THE GATES OF THE MUSEUM, Albert is reminded by the guard who accompanies him up the stairs that certainty about the past is not possible. Dressed in gold braids and brass buttons, the guard is bearish, large and old, he moves slowly and with discomfort. Halfway up the stairs he pauses for breath. He introduces himself as Boris. When he resumes the climb he says, "Certainty is a luxury no one can afford."

Albert has been invited to speak with the Director, have lunch with the Board, make a presentation to the Staff, as long as he agrees that historical certainty is acknowledged impossible. When Albert speaks to the Director over tea he comes directly to the point.

"I understand that someone has come to you claiming to possess bones of Adam and Eve?"

The Director is a middle-aged man with receding hairline and grey eyes in a smooth grey face. He is dressed in a dark, sharp-edged business suit. He sighs and looks away. "We have found two sets of human bone depositions. They could be those described in Genesis. An exact identification is impossible based merely on the evidence. A certain amount of faith is required. Still, what is not known is less significant than what is known, since the unknown is so

71

interesting but the known is always what has been agreed upon. The spirit of our blood is in our objects, a kind of life persists. We resonate with the past through the material objects created by our ancestors. These are significant artifacts, but exactly what they signify is always impossible to know with certainty. Ignorance, however, does not abolish our responsibility for their safe-keeping."

Albert pours more tea, adds sugar and stirs. "The newspaper reports have compounded the confusion. I suppose it is disheartening."

"The piece of clinching evidence," the Director says with an undisguised grimace, "purports to be the fossil remains of an apple in the female's skeletal hand." The Director sits back in his large chair and stares at a piece of chocolate-brown flint on his desk. "When I first came to this position I was an academic going nowhere in a profession going nowhere. Now, I am interviewed frequently. People ask my opinion. Do you understand? I enjoy the assurance that I am indispensable."

"So people actually believe that these could be the artifacts in question?"

"Though professionally I find the idea ludicrous, who am I to make the unsustainable assertion that these artifacts are not as claimed? Negative demonstration is impossible."

At the Board meeting Albert speaks enthusiastically of the work of the Museum and how impressed he is with the quality of its leadership. Later at the cocktail reception an elderly and distinguished Board member takes him aside. "We are not simply a research institution. We are responsible ultimately for all who enter this building, whatever their role or interest." The Board member looks to one side. "But we have a budget. The horns of our dilemma are oddly aligned. Since we cannot disprove these are the artifacts as speculated, why deprive our collections and our facilities of the support they may receive from those otherwise confirmed in such convictions? Disquieting as it may be, this attention has benefited our institution."

Albert smiles and walks slowly beside the Board member to a window overlooking the garden. "Doesn't it bother you that someone might think that because those objects are here, this attribution must be true?"

The Board member looks stricken, but then he smiles. "It is occasionally the case that one tolerates a particular and peculiar ignorance. Doing so permits the appropriate few to monopolize access to the artifacts themselves, and all of the profit such a monopoly inevitably makes available. This monopoly has allowed us to tolerate the withdrawal of support from those who take all of this perhaps too seriously and believe otherwise."

At the Staff meeting Albert expresses his enthusiasm for the work of the Museum and gratitude for the warmth of his reception. Later at the cocktail party a research staff member of considerable renown takes him aside. She is surprisingly young with a coquettish smile. "There are all kinds of scandalous materials stashed away in our basement. Bawdy material, if you get my drift. You'd be amazed by how much there is to be embarrassed about."

Albert says, "I understand there are large holdings of evidence of off-planet invaders in your collections. Some claim you have the artifacts to prove their existence as well."

Disappointed, the researcher shrugs. "Or at least do not disprove their existence. Our job is to argue frequently and agree rarely. Meanwhile, as speculation spirals about us, opportunities for the material support and growth of our institution increase. After all, without on-going research, a museum is merely a cool place full of neat stuff for rich people to display at parties. Significant support has recently been offered to expand our research into evidence for off-world contact in the Garden of Eden." Her eyes became large and she smiled. "Think of it: new staff, expanded building, perhaps even a new wing to the Museum. And think of the teaching opportunities. If the material in our collection can be identified as evidence of some cosmic visitation, our institution will become a world-center for this research. And think of all that might be added to our bank account. Speculation delights in its own wonder, and our efforts, no matter how well-substantiated, can at best only intensify the speculation of others."

Albert leaves the Museum gratified that while certainty is elusive, curiousity and wonder are still respected. Later he communicates his observations to the Mothership.

2

AT THE GATES OF THE MUSEUM, Albert is greeted by an Associate Curator carrying a fresh, white lab-coat, gloves and a mask. Albert has been invited to witness an event. He puts on the coat, gloves and mask.

Albert is led to a small windowless but well-lighted room, an examination table with appropriate apparatus at its the center. Beside Albert and the Director, there are three older men—the Curator and two Associate Curators—and three young women, apparently graduate students. They also wear lab-coats, masks and gloves.

A door at the end of the room opens, a cart appears pushed cautiously by two bulky young men, also apparently graduate students and recognizable despite their laboratory gear. On the top shelf of the cart encased in a translucent cube is a dull brown vase missing large pieces.

Albert and the others step aside as the young men push the cart to the edge of the examination table. With the help of the young women they lift the tray from the cart and place it in a recess at the center of the table. The Curator produces from his pocket a set of keys, uses them to turn certain locks and then lifts away the sides of the tray, leaving the encased vase anchored to the table.

From a compartment on the cart, one of the young men produces a sheaf of papers, and passes it to one of the young women. She glances through the file, separates several pages and then hands the rest to the other women who divide them among themselves. The largest file is handed to the younger Associate Curator. The older Associate Curator looks on. The Head Curator continues to gaze at the object. He steps to one side and then back in search of a different view. He brings his face so close to the encapsulating transparent cube his breath fogs its surface.

The older Associate Curator now speaks:

"The tests have been made and measurements done. The search of the historical record confirms what the chemical and mechanical tests report. Its motifs have been analyzed, its material composition has been identified. Its historical context has been recognized, its social significance deciphered, its significance and prestige have been noted. It has been weighed, photographed, measured and interpreted. Every observation about its appearance and essence has been recorded, duplicated, challenged and defended. Its commentary is extensive and subtle. Indeed, we have before us an object that is extremely old, made by hands long dead, looked upon by eyes long closed, for purposes long ago accomplished. Our ancestors made this, they honor us with this subtle gift, and now its presence honors us as we honor them."

The Associate Curator then hands a small bright brass key to the Chief Curator. The Chief Curator uses the key to turn a lock beside the tray on the examination table. With a hiss of entering air, the plastic capsule tips back. The

Chief Curator leans forward and gently grasps the vase. Cradled carefully in his hands he turns to the others.

"Lest their memory crumble to ash and be lost before the wind, let us pause and remember them and their achievements."

While the Chief Curator stands still, members of the party step forward, hands outstretched. Carefully he rests the vase briefly in the hands of each member. His hands extend just below those holding the object until it is passed back to him. Finally, Albert's turn arrives.

Albert considers deliberately dropping the vase. After a moment he hands it back to the Curator. When it is replaced on its stand, the capsule is moved forward and replaced on the tray.

Afterward there is wine and cheese in the Director's office. Albert realizes that in a subtle way he feels suddenly older and more profound. He is grateful for the experience and drinks too much. Later, Albert is scolded harshly by the Mothership for his inebriation and his delayed report.

3

AT THE GATES OF THE MUSEUM, Albert is introduced to Eric, the younger guard. Eric has less gold braid and fewer brass buttons than Boris. Albert is led by Eric down a series of wooden stairs to an old-style wooden-decorated office. Eric shows Albert around the room, pauses respectfully at various pieces of wooden office furniture. Albert reads small white cards placed on the pieces of furniture stating that this office has been used before by by a renowned scholar of no significance to the current members of the staff. Eric says nothing, appears utterly bored. Albert studies the furniture and reads the cards. The cards contain information pertaining to objects whose names and cultures he does not recognize.

Eric glances at his watch, then signals to Albert to follow. They follow a hallway to a staircase continuing down. In a room much like a carefully decorated basement Albert is greeted warmly by two Board members. The more elderly and heavy-set Board member seems to have trouble breathing. He shakes Albert's hand enthusiastically.

"So really good of you to come all this way. With your interest in our institution, we thought you might be willing to help us with a perplexing problem." He gestures Albert to a chair. Then he and the other Board member sit in chairs across from him. Between them is a low wide table with large sheets of paper marked and lined in pale blue.

The younger and apparently healthier Board member smiles and folds his hands. "We have received an enormous but anonymous grant to pursue the possibility of adding a new wing to the Museum dedicated to the display of our collection of artifacts of off- planet visitations. We realize you are a busy person but we hoped you'd give us advice on how the new wing might best be designed."

Albert folds his hands and crosses his knees. "Is the collection large?"

The older Board member clears his throat. "In addition to our own sizable collection, we are about to receive by anonymous donation a remarkable private collection of artifacts. These, we are assured, are authentic and positively dated. We believe it is our responsibility to the academic community and tax-paying public to display these artifacts and thereby demonstrate that their taxes are spent on useful and worthy science."

"Of course," the younger Board member adds, "we recognize that claims for these objects are not universally accepted. And at the moment we have yet to locate a curator for this collection. But we're confident that once we begin construction of this new wing we will attract a candidate capable of appreciating the quality of this collection, as well as its importance to the wider community. Eventually we expect to staff an entire department dedicated exclusively to the study of these artifacts and others identified from sites around the globe."

"Which is why," the older Board member injects breathlessly, "your help will prove so valuable. Eric introduced you to your new office. That office is itself a repository of history having been occupied by a remarkable succession of brilliant scholars before you. Unfortunately, all of them either committed suicide or went mad. We've had the office sprayed for vermin and viruses, but this is an old building. We have done our best to provide accommodations somewhat better than Spartan. Remember, glory has haunted that office, and must again."

"And glory in this case," the younger Board member says grinning, "will keep one eye on the budget." The two Board members stand and Albert stands with them. The men shake his hand warmly. Eric leads Albert back toward his office.

When they return to the office Albert discovers that it has been filled to the ceiling with books. Wooden boxes, stacks, piles; and all of them are books on architecture. Eric smiles at Albert and leaves locking the door behind him.

Albert finds himself locked in a room filled with books on architecture along with a desk and a chair. He ignores the books, sits down in the chair, puts his feet up on the desk, and waits until the light is turned off. Then he waits until the light is turned on again.

Some indeterminable time later Boris, the older guard, opens the door and shuffles into the room. Albert takes a book from the top of the nearest stack, turns to a page at random. "Here," he says offering the opened book to Boris, "tell them I've thought it over and I've decided the new wing should look like this."

Boris takes the book, nods once, and turns. He leaves the office with the door wide open. Albert stands. He finds the hallway abandoned. He is half way to the stairs when a voice calls out to him. Albert stops and turns. Boris, the older guard, eventually catches up to him. Panting he says, "The Board believes this design will exceed the budget for the project."

Albert smirks. "Tell them to calculate the difference in the cost and to contact my office in the morning with that figure. I'll have my secretary take it out of office petty cash."

Boris's eyes suddenly brighten. He straightens himself with a wide smile on his face. He lunges forward and embraces Albert. "We hoped you would say that." Tears appear in his eyes. "I have worked here all of my life, always hoping one day I would hear those words."

Albert follows Boris up the stairs. At the entrance to the Museum they are greeted by a crowd of cheering staff members. Visitors to the Museum stand by startled and amused by this incident. Albert is gratified to realize that he has added to the history of the material culture of this society, and that his efforts will be preserved for all future generations to contemplate and admire. The notion pleases him deeply.

Albert's report to the Mothership later that night is effusive although brief.

4

AT THE GATES OF THE MUSEUM, Albert is greeted by the Director. The Director invites him to examine the head of an extraterrestrial being. It is a dead being's head.

The dead being was discovered in an ancient Egyptian tomb and had been there a long time. The Director explains that while the head remains, its accompanying body mysteriously disappeared soon after discovery.

When they reach the laboratory, Albert steps close to the being's head and examines it carefully. He studies the ears and how the skin hangs from the neck.

The Director grins. "A remarkable acquisition, don't you think? Just look at the preservation of detail. And it is almost entirely intact. Even the color of the flesh is nearly life-like.

"This is no extra-terrestrial being," Albert announces.

The Director recoils with consternation. He questions Albert. Albert remains firm.

The Director says, "The field report accompanying this artifact states clearly the condition and situation of its discovery." The Director's grey eyes sharpen onto Albert.

Albert congratulates the Director for possessing a remarkably accurate counterfeit of an extra-terrestrial's head, but that it is a counterfeit nonetheless. Albert confesses a secret and overwhelming obsession with extra-terrestrial beings and their artifacts. And he assures the Director that he is even now preparing to add to his already substantial commitment of material support to the Museum's holdings in extra-terrestrial beings. But he must be assured of the integrity and scholarship of the research he supports. Then he explains all the ways one can recognize someone who is an extra-terrestrial being. Albert lays particular emphasis on the right ear, and how extra-terrestrial beings always have this little folded part just in the back. This, Albert explains, is how extraterrestrial beings recognize each other in any situation. Albert invites the Director to examine the head of this faux-extra-terrestrial being. After a moment the Director admits that he finds no ear-flap of the sort Albert describes behind the right ear of the being's head. "Just as I concluded," Albert says.

At Albert's request, the Director gives the fraudulent head to Albert in exchange for a check bearing numerous zeros. Albert promises to say nothing of the misidentification. The Director is relieved and thanks him for his discretion.

Later by tele-transport the head is returned to the Mothership where it is rejoined to the rest of the body for revivification. The Mothership extends greetings and expressions of gratitude for Albert's successful efforts.

5

AT THE GATES OF THE MUSEUM Albert is met by a handsome young woman. She informs him that she is the New Director. Somehow word got out; the previous Director's inability to recognize the fraudulent extra-terrestrial being's head cost the institution severely. There was nothing left for the Board to do but fire the previous director.

"Mind you," the New Director whispers, "I can hardly say I blame my predecessor. The pressure of this job is enormous." The New Director goes on to explain that the former Director failed to grasp the opportunities for aggressive marketing as they became available, but that this is precisely her forte. Albert is impressed by her energy and concentration and casual use of the French language. He offers his hand in congratulation, assures her of his continuing dedication to the aims and goals of the Museum. It occurs to Albert then, that it is time to go.

The New Director smiles with gratitude. "It was my hope that you would continue to support us." She takes his hand, grasps it warmly between her own.

"Because we now need your support even more than ever." The New Director reveals to Albert that negotiations are underway for a collection of newly-discovered books by Homer, Aristotle and Plato. The Museum has been greatly flattered by being the first institution offered such exceptional and rare works. Albert expresses mild surprise that there are still such undiscovered manuscripts in Greece. The New Director blushes beautifully.

"Actually, these are being carefully transcribed for us by a clairvoyant from Milwaukee. Fifth-century Athens has channeled its thoughts directly into her mind, she has been accumulating these documents for more than a decade. But our experts assure me that the woman has transcribed matters and languages she could have no other way of knowing. For this reason they can only be genuine"

"Actually," Albert says, "Homer is more 8th to 7th century, if I remember correctly. But I see your point." Even as he speaks Albert remembers that no good ever results from attempting to inform the ignorant.

"Our specialists are confident these documents are virtually genuine." The New Director makes this assertion with exciting self-assurance.

Albert congratulates the New Director on her remarkable sagacity as well as her luck. "And just think of the marketing opportunities."

The New Director says, "If we were not confident they were nearly authentic, we would never have approached you for support. The owner of the manuscripts insists that we build a new wing to the Museum to house the documents and to provide facilities for their decipherment and study."

Albert nods approvingly, even as he tries to recall the direction of the nearest exit. He assures her that he will be happy to help, but that unfortunately he will soon be leaving for Nigeria to review his holdings in gold and oil. Albert always feels better when he's come to a decision. He promises that he will leave word with his secretary, and the New Director can depend on him. The secretary in question has already been told by Albert to take no calls from the Museum or its New Director. A gentleman always knows when its time to leave a party.

The New Director flushes with excitement and relief. "Thanks," she says, "this job just has so much pressure. I've never felt under so much pressure." In a secluded hallway the New Director takes his arm, suddenly directs him into a corner. She leans forward and whispers, "And now I even have enemies. Isn't that exciting?"

"That is extremely exciting," Albert admits. "Do you have many enemies?"

"Not yet," the New Director says, "but there's always tomorrow."

"And are your enemies dangerous?"

The New Director seems suddenly cautious. "I don't really know. I've never had enemies before."

Albert acknowledges that he can understand her confusion. "But have you formed a plan to deal with these enemies?"

The question seems to elude the New Director. Albert brings to her attention the plays of Shakespeare and remarks how instructive they are in their depictions of enemies and their care and feeding. "Do you think your enemies are very much like Shakespeare's?"

The New Director of the Museum pauses. "I didn't know he had enemies," she says with some surprise. "Anyway, mine are not nearly that old and all of them speak English, which presents something of a challenge. But the conviction is gradually growing inside me that these enemies may actually be extra-terrestrial." She moves even closer to Albert, her breath caresses his eyelashes. "I believe they may actually be an extra-terrestrial hit-squad intent on capturing me and doing all sorts of odd sexual experiments on my body."

Albert asks what she will do. The New Director shrugs. "Probably something awful but necessary. I will sacrifice even my body to preserve this institution." The New Director shakes her head, smiles a weary smile that is embarrassing by its sincerity. "The job of being director isn't as easy as it looks. It's a lot like an iceberg."

Albert offers a quizzical glance, almost sad that the moment of departure has arrived. He wishes he could stay around and see how her encounter with her extra- terrestrial hit-squad turns out.

"A really big iceberg," the New Director continues. "You know, mostly invisible and all that. What makes this job so difficult is the iceberg quotient."

Albert smiles as he shakes her hand. Relieved that he will never see her again, Albert claims a pressing engagement, begs her leave, and advises her that for her own good, and the good of her institution, she should stay out of the sun.

ON THE MATTER OF DEATH

THERE'S TOO MUCH stuff that's alive around me and I'm pretty fed-up.

There's the guy next door who screams at his wife and kid, and who scream right back at him, these people remain alive and there's shit I can do about it. The dog that the guy across the street locks outside in his patio, this little rat-shit dog barks. Rain? It's out there. Snow? You got it. The old crazy woman down the block can't walk five feet insists she can drive her car nose right up to her door blocking our narrow street for hours. These pieces of Mother Nature's finest joke, these recycled effluences of organic floweration, these I must let live. But the cockroach behind the baseboard, the ants in the upper left cabinet, the mouse inside the stove, the mold on the bathroom shower tile, those vile creatures lurking around the rim of my toilet bowl, the bacteria, oh, the bacteria!, around my kitchen sink?

You are mine!

To these I am Doktor Doom, I am the Grim Reaper, I am the Force from the Next Dimension, I am their Worst Nightmare. A large responsibility and a tremendous challenge, it's true. And opportunities for failure lurk around every corner. But science and technology along with my own ingenuity have given me an arsenal of complexity and power.

That cockroach behind the baseboard can hide all he wants, fit himself into the smallest space, call on all his cockroach buddies to help and protect him, can pray the Cockroach Rosary and say countless Cockroach Novenas, but when my finger hits the button on that spray-can of poison, future cockroach generations evaporate because chemistry rules all. If only I could deal with the family next door that efficiently.

And those ants in the cabinet? Being smaller than a cockroach is likely an asset somewhere, but not here. Scattered everywhere or clustered into a tight knot, I always find them. But for those I don't, I've bought these little flat tins with openings in the sides that draw them in like teenagers to an internet porn site. Science never rests particularly when it comes to killing stuff.

That community of living, eating and fornicating creatures on the bathroom tile that looks just like a rust-stain? Nothing could be easier. And the best part? When you're just part of a shit-stain, no one can hear you scream.

Speaking of screams, let me tell you about those invisible monstrosities camped under the rim of the toilet. What good thing can be said in favor of creatures who hang out where I shit? Do they possess lofty aspiration, high goals, profound ambitions? Are they preoccupied thinking deeply, feeling powerfully, experiencing profoundly? Okay, so some of us don't live where we wished we lived or in circumstances we can control. And all right, so most of us make bad choices most of the time. Besides all that, among the few of us who understand, even fewer are able to use that understanding to their own advantage. I have begun to suspect that these creeps actively choose their creepiness just for creepiness-sake, pure and simple. But they die by the sheer power of my disgust and powerful caustic solvents, chemistry uber chemistry.

Those villainous nasties surrounding my kitchen sink are even worse. At least the toilet creeps have the good sense to hide, to disguise their shame, or at least not admit it. But the creatures around the sink? Their villainy is compounded by arrogance and a brazen indifference to being seen. As if they had some cosmic permission to add filth to my personal kitchen and shit where I eat. Like my kitchen sink was their beach resort. Over these creatures my power is absolute, and I exercise it without conscience. Yes, if all of us live to die, these live for me to kill. And I do it gleefully.

The mice, however, gives me pause. Maybe I watched too much Disney as a kid or maybe I took Mighty Mouse way too seriously. Maybe I look into their mouse eyes until I believed they look back, and in this way assume there's some sort of consciousness way back inside there that's more than simple animation. I suspect that all of this was the reason our first confrontation was so conflicted, and so unsettling.

My girlfriend, who is no longer my girlfriend, alerted me to their presence first by screaming, then by leaping onto the couch. Her reaction, as melodramatic as it was, is not the reason she is no longer my girlfriend, and I am no longer her boyfriend. Having disposed of her in the conventional non-lethal way I realized that this mouse and I needed to talk. If I ever acquired another girlfriend I did not want to be forced to make formal introductions.

So when the creature made its next appearance in my kitchen in a narrow space beside the stove, I turned off the overhead lights and squatted down onto the floor. I figured I'd do him the favor of informing him of the True Facts of Life.

"Here's the deal," I said. "Whether you know it or not this is where I live and you're not supposed to be here. And since you pay no rent, it's up to me to decide whether you'll remain my guest or not. And since I'm attempting to be honest, I'll confess that my temptation is to crush your skull under my heel. But I'm determined to be a nice guy. I've never succeeded at that, but I still try. So I figure if I give you the lay of the land, you'll recognize the hint and take it. So here I am, man to mouse, telling you that you need to know in order to take my suggestion seriously. Otherwise only really bad things will happen."

I waited. It was only fair to give that creature a chance to consider, to weigh options and then react and convince me not to do the thing I'm determined to do. So I waited. No surprise, this dim-wit mouse didn't offer so much as a squeak in his own defense. Not that I was entertaining contradiction. But I still wanted to be clear.

"Look, I don't go into your house and shit on your dinner plates, do I? Or munch holes into your food. Or embarrass you in front of your guests. And I definitely don't suddenly pop out and scare the shit out of your mouse-girlfriend. I mind my own human- type business. So all I'm asking is that you mind your own mouse business. Where is any of that not fair? What about all that is so hard to understand? You must recognize this is a relationship that's not working, that was doomed from the start and has nowhere to go. You have to see that, don't you?"

I might as well have been talking to a cat. So I stood and stamped my foot. In a blink the mouse disappeared behind the stove. And I went to my thinking chair to think and perhaps to brood.

I was already uneasy about killing this mouse, but now that we'd had our brief though one-sided, conversation, we'd begun a sort of relationship. Which is its own trap and makes things all much more complicated. It's one thing to squash something that has hair and then flush it down the toilet. But it's a whole different thing to squash one you've had a conversation with. Not like I'm a big believer in it, but karma is karma, and considering some of the shit I've done, and haven't done, I've really got to think over any misery I'd be adding to the world. This may not seem obvious to you, and you're probably surprised I even think about that, given my inclination to stop life from living given a sufficient opportunity. And that's probably because you don't see yourself as a person who kills gleefully, or efficiently, or even urgently. And maybe this is the difference between you and me; you may see the dispersal of misery as regrettable but also inevitable. I also see the existence of misery as inevitable, but I remain determined to take responsibility for my portion of it personally. Or maybe you're as likely to crush a cockroach as sneeze, and are just as relieved by the one experience as the other. If that is the case, have I anywhere here suggested you are heartless? Absolutely not. If anything, I offer my admiration. You are comfortable with the great chain of murder, of our evolutionary ladder and all its holy rungs, and with the dead and discarded piled around its base. You recognize without reflection or doubt that the difference between a protozoa and a cockroach is enormous, but also profound. You are so clear about this distinction, it is all but a reflex. Me? I'm always ready to ignore a distinction regardless of whether or not it's true, real, or sustainable.

So after my conversation with the mouse I got myself busy thinking I was thinking.

There seemed to be two things I needed to think about. First, was there a method to rid myself of this hairy annoyance that fell short of execution? And if not, was there any real point in attempting to minimize suffering? And this question led to a series of speculations on the nature of mouse suffering. That is; is there any reason to believe that the suffering of a mouse in any way resembled my suffering, particularly when my girlfriend broke up with me because I have a mouse in my house? Or in comparison to my suffering from a hangover after having drunk myself into a stupor over the fact that my girlfriend had dumped me because of my mouse problem? I mean, when I bang my big toe on the corner of my bureau, is what I endure in any way similar to what a mouse suffers when he's gotten caught in a glue-trap? Is a glue-trap a mouse-version of a broken heart?

I'm sure that really smart people out there have attached electrodes to various creatures' parts and then measured something they believed was important and which told them something. I remain unimpressed. I believe that anything measured instantly becomes unimportant. Submit to a test? Better you should cut my feet off and then see if they walk by themselves. Only so much measurement gets you knowledge, but it can never generate wisdom. Heisenberg was right in ways that none of us is ready even to consider.

But let me get back to my mouse, he's getting lonely and hates being ignored.

Specifically, the turmoil and self-doubt which resulted from our brief and unproductive conversation. Because the result was less clarity for me, not more. This mouse had not yet become a person, but it was rapidly drifting away from total anonymity. My reflections also reminded me that I'm far from knowledgeable about the love-life of a mouse. So I would need to be satisfied with a trial-and-error approach.

Given the conflicted nature of our relationship, I decided to attempt non-violent discouragement. So I tried post-its first. I stuck them along the kitchen baseboard so they'd all be at mouse-eye level. I wanted to be emphatic and creative but non- threatening. So I wrote things like, "Life is better lived outdoors," and, "Fresh air is your birthright." One I thought particularly clever was, "Take care of yourself and your grandchildren will thank you." Upbeat and encouraging without being sentimental. Another I liked was, "Do you know where you'll be tomorrow?" Not nearly as good, kind of existential, and yet immediately urgent. This all took the better part of a day, and by dinner time I'd posted all of them. After that, there was only the need to wait.

And I did not need to wait long. Out of the corner of my eye I watched the mouse appear beside the stove. And sure enough, he crawled slowly along the baseboard in the kitchen checking out my messages. I was flattered. If no one has told you, it's easy to catch the attention of a mouse, but it's difficult to hold it, and it is even tougher to get one to read your stuff. I waited to give him a chance to take their unsubtle hint. But it was just my luck to have a mouse who was a slow reader and it took him more than half an hour to take it all in. But finally he must have finished because when I looked again he was gone.

I decided that, given the sophistication and care I'd put into my messages, surely this mouse was now considering his life-options and had already begun to pack his things. Imagine my surprise the next evening when I spotted him again, and his packed bags were nowhere to be seen. I thought of all sorts of reasons why his departure might be delayed. If this mouse needed excuses

I was ready to give him a carton of them. But that didn't appear to be his problem. I was annoyed but I was determined to avoid being angry; it never gets me anything except more trouble. I stepped into the kitchen and to the mouse I said, "I took a lot of time coming up with those slogans. The least you could do is think them over." But this mouse had nothing to say, so I stamped my foot, causing him to disappear, and then I went back to my brooding chair. Not that it mattered. My options were disappearing along with their alternatives. Still, I was determined to leave murder as the last recourse.

I wondered if an escalation of messages might help, so I replaced the post-its with more urgent ones. Unsubtle messages like, "Get out or die!" and, "Death is more patient than your mother," and, "Flight sheds no blood." It seemed our relationship had progressed far beyond the hinting stage.

It took a while but I finished the new messages and posted them the following evening. And I didn't need to wait long. By the time I'd sat down in my brooding chair the mouse was already out and reviewing those messages. And I guess they were so straightforward the mouse made the rounds quickly. At the end he sort of froze. I watched him certain he was about to move, but he didn't. So then I wondered if we needed another heart-to-heart. I wasn't optimistic, but I was determined to explore every option.

With the lights turned off I got down on the kitchen floor again. I said, "I know this is difficult to understand, but my patience has run out and that's a bad thing. From your perspective you've found a spot you won't give up without a battle. But I'm here to tell you, don't kid yourself. This is not the place you want to be, and I am not the person you want to cross. Don't mistake patience for cowardice, buddy. You're living on borrowed time and I'm the timekeeper."

This stupid mouse just huddled there beside the stove. I thought that any second he'd disappear, but it was like he was drugged or hypnotized. As though my messages had stunned him into catatonia. Still, I wanted to give him the most latitude, so when I'd finished my speech I stood, stamped my foot and watched as he woke up and scurried away. I was a little relieved when he left. I was beginning to wonder if he'd already died of fright.

Again I thought it was important to give the little creep a chance to absorb the messages and proceed accordingly. So I paid no attention to him for twenty-four hours, long enough for him to deliberate, consult, and then pack. In fact, during that time about the only thing I thought about was a plan for when the mouse ignored the latest warning. As unlikely as it is to explain, death was creeping up on both of us.

The next night came and went without an appearance by the mouse, and foolishly I began to congratulate myself on my success. I thought this might be one situation where Death does not win. At least not immediately. So that night I slept pretty well. But this life is brutally efficient at the extermination of illusions. The next night set me straight on my power over the behavior of this mouse. He made his appearance a bit later than usual but suddenly there he was, as if we'd never talked, as if he hadn't read my messages, as if there had never been any messages for him to read. Eyes blinking and whiskers twitching, you'd wonder if he was an entirely different mouse.

How could I explain to this mouse, whichever mouse it was, that my dark side was coming out, that his time was running out with it, and that his executioner was already at the door? All my messages, all my efforts, all my patience, had only made his aspiring murderer more bloodthirsty. So I brought out my weapon, my one and only big gun, a blunt instrument but guaranteed to get the job done. When the mouse was clearly unimpressed by my threats I went into the kitchen, sat on the floor and said, "Okay, here it is, ready to go. Either you leave, or you deal with this." And in my hand I waved a two-pack of glue traps. "I know you can read," I said, "but even if you can't, you can certainly recognize pictures."

From the mouse's reaction I might just as well have been waving the Sunday New York Times crossword puzzle at him. I said, "They say it's best to greet Death with a smile. Think you can do that for me?" For all the reaction I got I could have been a concrete pillar.

But I knew the secret, even if the mouse didn't. Peanut butter, better than mouse cocaine. A quarter of a teaspoon placed at the center of the trap and any mouse was doomed. It had as little chance of avoiding this trap as I could avoid paying taxes. After another moment's thought I decided to give the mouse one more night of freedom. "Call all your girlfriends and live it up," I told the mouse, "because tomorrow you die."

Next afternoon I set a half-dozen traps at either end of the kitchen and in places the mouse couldn't avoid. Just after the sun went down I turned off all the lights and left my apartment for a bar I've sometimes gone to. My hope, of course, was to live it up too, before I'd put one more smirch on my shaggy, raggedy soul, and maybe even meet someone who'd pretend to be my girlfriend for at least one night. I was not optimistic, and probably did myself grave injury when I told every person who came near me of my plan for my mouse and the havoc that plan would create. But optimism has never been a prerequisite. I was determined to close the bar, and thus give my mouse the maximum chance to off himself, unaided by my hands. At least in any direct way.

By the time I returned to the apartment I was drunk as shit, but that didn't matter.

Sobriety would not have helped in this adventure.

As I predicted, when I entered the apartment and headed toward the kitchen I could already hear the squeals of distress. What I had not expected was that two traps were occupied by unwilling guests. I had not caught one mouse, but two. I sat down on the floor and considered the misery I was now responsible for, even more misery than I'd bargained for. It's hard to describe my emotions at the time.

Those tiny black pin-head eyes darted from me to the narrow space beside the stove the mice had expected to use as an exit. One had the side of its face stuck fast to the glue so that the other eye had no choice but to look up and around at me, the other's chin and throat were caught fast, allowing it to squeal and squeal but for no good purpose.

Sitting in the middle of the kitchen floor and halfway between each I said, "Okay, guys, what I have attempted to avoid, you have rushed toward like Fate. I would have had this end in a very different way, but here we are, and so be it. If I had one wish, it would be that all mice hear your anguish, and learn thereby. Not that I believe that's likely, or even possible, but it is my genuine wish, for all that may be worth. Do your mouse-buddies a favor and get the word around."

As I think about it now I have no idea why I said any of this. Most likely it was my bad conscience, my deformed and corrupt conscience, or something I'm stuck with that's very much like a conscience. Or the fact that I was still pretty drunk.

Having captured my prey there was now the issue of disposal. Most people in my situation find this even more difficult than the capture. Not me. Maybe I was just drunk enough, but I simply pulled out a plastic bag, tossed both traps with their occupants inside, tied off the top and dropped the bag from my fourth-floor window into the alley. Murder, I have always believed, must be irresponsible, and I was utterly unconcerned with what might happen to my bag of soon-to-be-dead mice.

Anyway, I think this is the end of my story. I think I've explained life and death and how one gets to be the other, and how I have functioned within that process. I've explained my role and how I see myself in that role, how that role is a particularly good one for me no matter how reluctant my participation, because I didn't participate until I was powerfully provoked, and how a role becomes inevitable. And I think I've made it clear that, really, I'm pretty comfortable with all of this. I'm even ready to take over the responsibility for others. And that's pretty generous of me, although I don't expect gratitude. And I most certainly don't want to be paid for it. After all, what kind of person do you think I am?

JEFFREY'S LIFE ON TV

JEFFREY WATCHED two amber-red cockroaches walk in opposite directions across the laundromat floor. The cracked black & white linoleum was thinly covered with a haze of lint and small pale bits of paper. His battered yellow plastic chair gave him a perfect view of his laundry spinning lazily inside the dryer. And then the man walked in. Jeffrey was alone in the laundromat and the man walked directly to him.

"Give you two tokens for a dollar," the man whispered.

The tokens ran the washers and dryers and they cost twenty-five cents from the vending machine ten feet from where Jeffrey sat. The man looked crazy enough and Jeffrey did not want to argue, so he handed the man a dollar bill and told him to keep the tokens.

The man yelled, "I don't take no goddamn charity," threw the tokens at Jeffrey and left. One struck him just above the eye.

Eventually Jeffrey's clothes got dry.

With his clothes in a sack slung over his back he climbed the stairs to his apartment where to his distress he found his front door wide open. Jeffrey lived alone and he distinctly remembered locking the door before he left. Still carrying the laundered clothes, Jeffrey walked directly into his living room. To his astonishment, he discovered a new, larger television sitting in the place of his old one. Nothing else in the apartment seemed disturbed, nothing appeared missing. And there was this new tv. He did not call the police.

He went to his bedroom, emptied the sack of clothes still hot from the dryer onto his bed, returned to the living room and turned on the television. The television worked perfectly, the image and the color and sound were all crystal sharp. But it took a moment to realize he did not recognize the program he was watching. Jeffrey flipped from channel to channel without seeing a program, a face, a commercial product or even a corporate logo that he recognized. He stood and looked behind the television.

The only wire attached to the back of the tv ended plugged into the wall-outlet. There was no visible antenna, no satellite dish or cable line. He returned to the couch and flipped back through the channels. Now he saw even more programs, and there were faces he did not remember having seen the first time through the channels.

And there were the sports. Games he did not recognize were being played by rules he could not decipher on fields of bizarre proportion. And he saw game shows in which contestants did things for indeterminable reasons to the inexplicable guffaws and cheers of invisible studio audiences. Even the news broadcasts were about countries he had never heard of. He stood again and looked over the back of the television more carefully.

This time he noticed a small white sticker advising him to call a certain phone number if he had any problem with the device. He called.

"Jeffrey!" The pleasant male voice addressed him with shrill pleasure, as if he had been waiting for Jeffrey to call. "How do you like your new television?"

"I don't," Jeffrey said.

"You don't what?" The voice was suddenly thick with startled disappointment.

"There's something wrong with it. I can't figure out where these programs come from. I can't understand anything that's going on."

"But our programs are all in English. That's your language of preference, right? So how can this be?"

"I don't have a problem with the language. But I don't understand anything else. I've never seen any of this before."

"But we thought that was what you wanted. You said you were fed-up, bored. So we gave you what you said you wanted, something new. An infinitely-various television. Because we thought this would please you."

When Jeffrey said nothing, the voice continued. "This is what we technically refer to as a scramble television. It takes all the in-coming signals from all the in-coming television shows and it mixes them together like scrambled eggs. Plot-points from one show are blended with characters from another show and the dialogue from still another show and a setting for even another show. This wonderful device even rearranges the eyes of one actor with the lips of another actor, the body of still another actor, the voice of another, and the hair and clothes of still another."

"Well, I can see where this might improve things," Jeffrey said with more sarcasm than conviction.

"That's precisely our intention: improvement. This is break-through technology. This is the leading edge of the next generation. We've been watching you, Jeffrey, and from the very beginning we recognized you as a perceptive viewer capable of appreciating the implications of our revolution. How many times have you grumbled that you hate watching the same boring-old-thing-television?"

"Well, if you're so good at this, how about doing something about my sex-life?"

"Too easy. Besides, this new video technology might even help you there, too."

"That seems unlikely."

"Jeffery, I'm going to be honest with you. This tv is so revolutionary even we, its creators, don't know exactly how it will affect people, or in what ways it will change their lives or how they perceive themselves. Because no two tv's are alike, we have no idea exactly what anyone is seeing. Turn two of them to the same channel at the same time and you will see two entirely different tv shows."

"And how is that an improvement? How will anybody know what program is coming on next, or after dinner, or after the evening news?"

"Isn't that precisely the point? The problem with boring television is that it is predictable, and that is because it is programmed. And it's programmed to receive programs. Everything is programmed. Everything is a program. In fact, if it isn't a program, it isn't. It is precisely this predictability that remains its flaw. So we have attempted to perfect the unprogrammable television. You will never know whether you are watching a cop show or home shopping. You'll never know any difference because there will never be any difference. Every show will have some blood, a few boobs and a little bit of shopping. And if the show you're watching gets dull you can always change the channel until the show gets better. If you don't like the way a character looks just wait a little while, that character will look different on another channel."

After a pause Jeffrey said, "Can I call you back?"

"Of course," the voice said, "any time. Meanwhile, let me give you a hint. Turn to channel eighteen. Maybe we can kill two birds with one tv show." The voice gurgled a particularly vulgar laugh. The sound washed over his ear, Jeffrey endured a wave of nausea as he hung up the phone. But he did as he was told and tuned the television to channel eighteen.

Suddenly on the screen appeared a character looking exactly as Jeffrey would like himself to look. He is sitting under bright sunshine in the shade of a tree. The leaves of the tree and the grass around him are remarkably green. The small stream flowing beside him glitters. He can see two small amber-red fish swimming lazily near the shore. Jeffrey's character looks up, the camera follows his eyes, to see a perfectly even and unbearably bright blue sky, a blue Jeffrey has only seen on boxes of laundry detergent and coloring certain brands of mouth-wash. Jeffrey wonders what he is doing here, as Jeffrey sits in his living room wondering what he is doing there. Jeffrey grits his teeth as he sits in his chair, resisting the anticipation that something is about to happen. It occurs to him that the man on the phone might know more than he's admitting. And it also occurs to him that this tv might not be so unpredictable. But if that was the case, why did he give Jeffrey that story about the television? On the screen he sees a movement in the trees, the camera pans in close. Jeffrey on his couch sits forward, as Jeffrey on the screen turns toward the sound.

Two thick branches heavy with fat, iridescent green leaves part, a woman appears. Tall and elegant with abundant dark hair, she wears a pale blue high-collared dress that reaches down to her feet. Its narrow waist enhances her ample proportions. She seems to move just above the grass. Her posture is reserved yet her smile is as sweet as cheap breakfast cereal. Jeffrey believes he recognizes her, and then wonders at the nature of resemblance, and the resemblances of nature.

She sits down beside him. Propped on one arm she leans toward him. Her dark green eyes do not leave his, her smile does not fade. "It is so wonderful to finally be with you."

"Yes it is," Jeffrey says a little dazed. Jeffrey on the couch is amazed at the tv Jeffrey's ineptitude.

"We're all alone now," she says staring deeply into his eyes. "My father will never find us here."

Jeffrey on the tv nods and smiles. Jeffrey on the couch leans forward reaching for the channel selector.

The woman looks up to the sky as she reaches to her throat and unbuttons the first four buttons. "It is so warm," she says sighing, "I could just lie here and doze all day."

Both Jeffreys stare into cleavage deep and abundant.

"Me too," Jeffrey says. He smiles and looks away, as Jeffrey on the couch squirms.

"All of that laundry," she says, her voice heavy with astonished gratitude, "I never thought I would ever see anyone do so much laundry. Why, since I was born the dirty laundry has just piled up. Whole wings of our castle have been dedicated to the storage of stained and soiled laundry. Grass stains, tea and coffee, chocolate ice cream that refused to wash out. Rust, grease and tomato sauce. And worst of all, ring around the collar. We were lost, our kingdom prostrate with despair. But you arrived on your white horse. As if with a mere snap of your fingers we were saved. Now our kingdom has clothes that are bright and clean, and smell so fresh. Even Dad is astonished." Breathing heavily, bosom heaving she adds, "No man could ever do so much for me."

"Oh really," Jeffrey says grinning with embarrassment, "it was nothing. Honestly, I simply trusted my laundry detergent. Powerful yet gentle, and with the fresh smell of Spring. I'm just glad I could help."

The woman leans closer, her free hand caresses his cheek, she stares deeply into his eyes. An emotion passes through her, Jeffrey on the couch watches it cloud her face. "Would you make love to me?"

Jeffrey on the screen smiles brightly. "I'll do better than that. I will marry you."

As the Jeffreys watch, the woman's expression darkens. Suddenly a sparkling silver knife appears in her hand. "I don't need your goddamn charity," she says evenly and stabs him through the heart.

Jeffrey on the couch watched the knife rise and fall several times. He watched crimson blood arc and splatter from his wounded chest for a long while before finally he grabbed the remote and turned the tv off. Then he called the telephone number. It rang several times before the line opened, and Jeffrey heard heavy breathing but no greeting.

"Hey," Jeffrey said, "anybody there?"

"Of course," an impatient voice responded. "What do you want?" This voice was thicker and darker than the previous, and Jeffrey's curiosity was aroused.

"What happened to that other guy?"

"What other guy?"

"The other guy I was talking to."

"That would be me."

"Sorry, but you sound different."

"Don't worry about it. I have a head cold."

"But you didn't have a head cold a minute ago."

"It comes and goes. You know how it is. But enough of the chit-chat. You like that machine or what?"

"Well," Jeffrey said, "I have issues."

"Yeah?" the voice said. "Well, I have hemorrhoids. So get to the part where I care. I got to go to the head."

"I was just thinking maybe there's a way so I could get the channel where only the good stuff happens."

"You mean, sort of like the Good-Stuff-Happens channel?" The voice was sarcastically earnest.

"Well, I mean, yeah. I mean, what could it hurt for me to like win sometimes."

"Yeah," the voice said, its pause was pseudo-thoughtful. "I can see your point. Kind of like the Jeffrey-Wins channel."

"I mean I could just leave it on all the time. You know, kind of like getting to see myself win."

"Doing what?"

"Just what we were talking about."

"You mean winning? You?" The laughter leaking from Jeffrey's telephone was acid poured into his ear. He replaced the receiver and returned to his bedroom.

But as he stood over the jumbled pile of warm, clean laundry, he could feel the tv tugging at him. After all, he had looked good on the tv. His weak chin had been replaced with something firm and cleft. His cheeks were slimmer, not gaunt but determined, even hungry. As he folded his jeans he recalled something jaunty, almost swaggering, about his tv self. And that woman. Well, she kind of looked like his old girlfriend, except better. There has to be a version of the tv show where I don't always get stabbed. On some channel at some time, that tv Jeffrey will get the girl but without the knife. Maybe that version will play later tonight; maybe it's playing right now.

When Jeffrey finished folding his laundry he turned toward the living room, but at the doorway he stopped.

The absent tv left a palpable void. Jeffrey focused his eyes hard on the space where it had been, he studied the air that had once surrounded it. The tv-gone was even larger than the tv-present. Then he looked toward his front door. It took a moment to realize the door was slightly open. As if whoever had passed through it had not wanted the closing door to make a sound. Jeffrey went to the door and opened it wide, looked along the empty corridor in both directions almost relieved to see it empty. When he closed it firmly and locked it, he returned to the couch and to studying the empty tv space. As if a hole had been cut into the room, a single tooth missing from a grinning mouth. And they hadn't even returned his old one.

From the couch his gaze returned to the space where the tv had been. Jeffery stared at that space, scrutinized it, until a fascinated glaze fell over his eyes. Arms folded and feet on the low table before him, Jeffrey watched the blank space of the tv and wondered what he was doing now.

AT LOVE IN THE HOUSE OF WORK

OUR HOUSE IS actually a clock. One of those really big clocks you see in Europe on top of the town hall or some castle, where its face is as big as a garage door and the gears are bigger than trash cans. And even though we're certain we own this monster-clock- house, my wife and I circle its base writing checks, gesturing to ourselves and amusing others on the hour.

Eleanor is a physically small person, and I am not. She bought a house, I bought something closer to a rabbit's warren. Although it is all the same building, my wife and I live in different houses.

The inspector insisted the house was in good condition, but he must have looked only at Eleanor's house. In Eleanor's house things ran smoothly; in my house something always happened. In her house appliances worked with bright precision, appliances in my house cycled into continual sequential breakdown. Thus, after replacing a broken drive belt in the dryer, I discovered our perfectly running freezer frozen solid with glaciers flowing down the inside walls of the refrigerator and everything inside rock-hard. I promised myself I'd defrost the next day and went to the front door to lock-up. But a spring slipped inside the lock making that impossible. After a desperate phone call I sat up late waiting for the locksmith. While waiting I set the toaster to toast two pieces of bread and pressed the lever. Sitting in the living room minutes later, the smell of smoke brought me back into the kitchen. Small flames licked just at the top of the toaster.

When the locksmith finally arrived he sniffed. "Geez, smells like you had a fire in here."

"Do you know anything about toasters?" I asked.

He shrugged. "They burn bread. Don't you like burned bread? You're a homeowner now, you can enjoy your burned bread under your own roof. A roof I'll suggest you refrain from burning down. Especially while I'm under it." He repaired the lock and stood to leave but then he sighed as if I was the stupidest person he'd ever met. "Listen," he said, "a house is a cluster of interlocking systems. I'm surprised nobody bothered to tell you this secret. Bet you thought all you'd do is sign mortgage checks for thirty years. Enjoy your burned bread." He took my check and left.

I locked the door behind him and switched on the light in the dining room. The light flashed and then the first floor went dark. I recognized a suggestion and went upstairs to bed.

Before she left for work the next morning Eleanor asked, "How much is it going to cost?" I said it was a good thing nothing ever broke down in her house. She would save a lot of money that way. She would even become rich. "I'm careful," she responded, "and I take care of things, so things take care of me. How would you like a nice steak and baked potato for dinner tonight? And I'll bring home a bottle of red wine." The possibility that she might prepare dinner charmed me into silence. Her smile hung in the air when she had gone.

I checked in with Tracy, my office secretary, for phone messages and let her know I wouldn't be in. Then over the telephone I consulted a house psychologist. I said I thought I had an emergency and described what had been happening. The woman I spoke with was named Cathy and she agreed to meet me at the house at three that afternoon. She said she suspected severe schizophrenia and possibly a nervous breakdown. "A house is like a pet." She hesitated and then said, "Well, there are certain things we can try."

Cathy had a wonderful smile. She arrived wearing large glasses that gave her the look of a mischievous owl. In the breast pocket of her blouse she wore a plastic pen protector. Her blouse was tight, the pocket protector angled obliquely. She was tall and seemed a person who ought to be believed. I said, "My wife usually isn't home until after six."

She said, "We should probably start in the basement."

"We have plenty of time," I said, "start where you like."

I led the way down the steps. Beside the washing machine she brought out a small computer-like device with a cable and a kind of microphone attached to the end. She tapped keys on the small key-pad, a tiny screen lighted, she tapped the key pad again, then took the microphone device into her other hand.

"A house is a complex of interlocking systems. This device reads what we like to call the relative unhappiness quotient of various systems. Once we identify their locations, some kind of rehabilitation can begin. We can prepare for a better future." She held the microphone over the washer and then the dryer. "This device is collecting readings that I will down-load into the mainframe at my office. These measurements will take some time." Her skirt was snug, I enjoyed watching her move about. And I liked her smile a lot. I said, "I'd like to watch, if you don't mind. Maybe I'll learn something."

She took measurements on walls, pipes, wires, the floor, everything that connected with anything. Connections of wood, metal, glass, rubber, plastic, linoleum, concrete or any hybrid thereof. She was patient and thorough. I followed her up the stairs when she finished. Watching her was improving my day. My confidence in Cathy grew, I felt optimistic.

In the dining room she held the device over glasses and china. "I can pick up smudges of discontent, sort of fingerprints on the crystal stem-ware of life."

In the kitchen she took considerable time taking readings at the refrigerator and dishwasher. "Unhappiness is an incomplete connection between two semi-autonomous but interlinked systems. Incompleteness persists all around us. Our systems collect residual unhappiness and complex systems concentrate and amplify it. High levels of instability result in mechanical breakdown. This dishwasher, for example. Its break- down is immanent. You might get a couple of days out of it, but that's all."

"Shouldn't we do something?" I asked.

"We are," she said. "We're taking measurements." I liked her smile more and more.

In the living room she spent a lot of time taking measurements over the couch and around the stereo system. "Do you play this system very loud?" she asked. When I said I didn't she seemed perplexed. "We should take measurements upstairs," she said.

"After you," I said. There were more stairs to the second floor than from the basement. My day continued to improve.

In the bathroom she said, "System stresses frequently collect in the plumbing. Had any trouble with your flush?" When I said I hadn't she seemed puzzled. "The principles of fluid dynamics raise fundamental questions about the membrane that separates organized from chaotic systems. Believe me," she said kneeling beside the toilet, "the movement of fluids through a house is a complex equalization of pressure and gravity. Plumbing is the system most vulnerable to sensitivity dependence on initial conditions. Just clog up a toilet with paper and flush."

I nodded. "Initial conditions are everything." I understood.

We went into the small guest room beside the bathroom that Eleanor uses as a study. Cathy took a number of measurements over and around the guest bed, tapped several keys in the key pad. "Knots of incoherence." She tapped more keys and casually asked, "Do you and your wife make love on this bed?"

"No," I said, unsure I'd given the correct answer.

Cathy simply shook her head. "Time to check the master bedroom."

She worked carefully making measurements over our bed. When she finished taking readings over the rest of the furniture, she sat down on the edge of the bed. I sat down beside her.

"I'll know better after I've run the program but I'm getting elevated levels of discordance in several places. Primary systems are critically close to avalanche breakdown, where one or more systems interlock destructively with other systems. If you don't mind my professional speculation, my readings suggest you don't use this bed for much more than sleeping." If there's a good response to that speculation it didn't come to mind. "We need to break up these nodules of incompletion one by one. So far your problems have been mere annoyances. But suppose your heater exploded or your washer overflowed or your dryer caught fire? Angry houses can kill." Her mouth was grim and hard-set. "What we're trying to avoid is nothing less than homicide by domicile."

I was convinced. She said, "I suggest we start in the guest room." She stood, I followed.

Beside the guest room bed she began to unbutton her blouse. "This will be only an initial treatment, a sort of patch." She removed her skirt. "Your house will need several treatments. But computer analysis will give us clearer direction." When she'd removed the rest of her clothes she laid down. Then she looked up at me. "We should probably get started."

At one point she said, "Slow down." Later she said, "My work puts me at the center of points of energy transfer. Quanta of energy cascade into near-stable systems generating standing waves that block energy transference. By this generation of wave patterns out of phase with the standing wave, energy is released and energy levels leap to the previous stable state, thus permitting free energy transfer. I love my work." Later she said, "Hurry now." She was a person who knew what she was doing and this impressed me.

After we'd dressed she handed me her business card. "That's my emergency number. Next time a system breaks down, call me. Day or night. I need readings of systems in break-down state for a complete analysis. I'll be here as quickly as possible." I promised I'd keep her informed.

When Eleanor arrived home from work I told her I was getting a handle on the break-down problem. She said, "Good", and then she sighed and handed me a small brown paper bag. "Sorry about dinner," she said, "but work was so crazy." Inside the bag was a half-bagel and a Reeses Peanut Butter Cup. I smiled and shrugged.

"Don't worry," I said frustrated that there would be no nice steak and baked potato with red wine tonight, and then fixed a meal of pasta and jar pasta sauce. But nothing broke down that night until very late. Eleanor had already gone to bed. I put dishes into the dishwasher, added soap and turned it on. The machine went through the fill cycle but then stopped. I made sure I had done everything but the machine would not re-start. I brought out her business card and called Cathy.

"I thought this afternoon's treatment would have taken care of that," she said over the phone. "False alarms will cost you." I assured her that this was not a false alarm. She promised to come right over.

Minutes later she knocked quietly at the front door. "Show me," she said walking past me toward the kitchen. She did not stop to take off her coat.

At the dishwasher she brought out a device that resembled the other, but was larger and different. After tapping the key-pad several times she attached a cable to the dishwasher and another to a glass full of water. "Water is the perfect conductor of feed- back. It provides the path by which unhappiness in one part of the world generates unhappiness in others." She tapped more keys, paused and then tapped more keys.

"Your mechanical systems," she continued, "are out of phase with your plumbing system. You've got serious sequential convergence problems." She tapped more keys and then leaned forward over the dishwasher. "I'm going

to need your help." She lifted her coat and then her skirt over her back. Over
her shoulder she said, "Let me know when you're ready." When I said I was
ready she tapped more keys on the key pad. "Hurry," she said. Then she said,
"Harder." When I responded she tapped more keys on the key pad. "To the
left," she said. I adjusted. "More," she said, and I complied. Then she said,
"Harder," and then, "Hurry," which I did. "Now," she said. With a loud clank
the dishwasher suddenly began to work. When she'd caught her breath she
tapped more keys, then disconnected the wires. "You shouldn't have any more
problems with this machine. At least for a while." She wound the wires around
the device. "Wait until the dishwasher cycles through before you go to bed
tonight, just to make sure." The beeper on her belt went off; she tipped it and
glanced at the display. "Got to run. I'll call as soon as I've down-loaded this
data and finished the analysis." She smiled and then she was gone. I liked
that smile more and more. The dishwasher worked properly and then I went
upstairs. Eleanor snored contentedly.

Nothing else broke down. Days later as she was leaving for work Eleanor
offered to make fettuccine Alfredo for dinner. I told her I looked forward to
it. Just before lunch Cathy called me at my office. We agreed to meet at the
house, and an hour later she knocked at the door.

She walked in with a rolled chart in her right hand. "C'mon and take a
look," she said over her shoulder. She unrolled the chart on the dining room
table, leaned over it with her hands on her hips and grinning. The chart
displayed circles of various sizes and different primary colors. Dominated by
a large yellow circle, there were several small red circles, three of them were
inside the yellow circle, several more small green circles and one very small blue
circle. Inside and outside the circles in small neat printing were numbers and
formulas and symbols and words like "living" and "dining" and "sitting." And
criss-crossing everywhere were thin black lines.

"The computer has tracked the emission patterns of various sub-atomic
particles. By correlating the distribution of gravatinos and gluons, and
combining this with a map of leptron concentrations, we're able to chart the
probability of weak-force dissipation. Without a smooth and consistent transfer
of the weak force things fall apart. Thus, in these red areas the weak force
has reversed polarity, while in the blue the dissipation has reached maximum
efficiency according to Planck's constant and the inverse ratio of baryon-to-
meson accumulation. But this only gives us momentary relationships. To

calculate the temporal evolution we track tachyon particles for possible FTL signaling. That's what the lines and the numbers are about. They indicate temporal fields through which weak-force accumulations shift. It traces a sort of time-tunnel through which the weak-force fields are advancing temporally."

I said, "Isn't that something. Who would have thought?"

Cathy grinned proudly, her owlish glasses glinted in the weak light. "Advances in quantum theory have made all of this possible. We're lucky to be living in this century."

"So where should we start?" I asked. I had to look away.

"There are serious rifts in the front room upstairs, the bathroom, and in the basement. We should take care of those today. I'll come back to take measurements and see how the pattern re-alignments are progressing. We'll go from there."

"Fine," I said.

Chart in one hand and device in the other she led the way up the stairs. I liked following her. The first room was the master bedroom. She put the chart on the bed and turned on another device, one I hadn't seen before. She held it over the bed and studied the screen, then referred to the chart. She put the device on the bureau, rolled up the chart, and began to unbutton her blouse. "Readings are all as I expected." When she'd undressed she laid across the width of the bed. "Wait," she said and brought out a compass. "We need to align across the earth's gravitational field." When she found the correct position we aligned.

She said, "Right there," and "That's it," and "Harder," and "Slow down," and then "Hurry." I did what was necessary.

Afterward we lay on our stomachs panting like marathon runners. She clapped me on the shoulder saying, "That wasn't too hard. We'll lick this thing." I could only nod and smile. Then she stood.

"We'd better get going." She glanced at her watch. "Temporal continuity is critical." With the chart and the device she walked naked into the bathroom. From the bed I watched her spread the chart on the floor and then check her device. "This is the spot," she said, "right here." She stood in a corner of the shower.

I stood on weak knees and went to stand beside her. With attentive assistance we did what needed to be done. Immediately afterward she referred to her device for more readings. "Excellent," she said panting, strands of her pale hair laid sweat-plastered to her forehead.

"I need a break," I said, walked back to the bed and laid down.

Cathy checked her watch. "Eight minutes," she said.

"Would ten minutes be cutting things too close?"

"The displacement of large numbers of sub-atomic particles creates subtle shifts in the temporal field. By adhering to the appropriate rhythm we avoid leaks or tears in the temporal fabric. And we are engaged in major particle displacements. We're moving sub-atomic universes. Besides, getting this last one right is critical to the efficiency of the previous two." She stretched her arms above her head. I became inspired. She checked her watch again and stood.

She carried the chart and device, I followed her down the stairs until we were in the basement. There she opened the chart on the floor and scrutinized the device. She stood between the washer and dryer and gas heater and said, "This is it." With another glance at her watch she said, "We'd better hurry."

Grasping the rafter overhead she stood with her feet wide apart. I needed more help which she patiently donated as I embraced her from behind. Again she glanced at her watch and said, "Hurry." I followed her direction until she said, "There, right there, just like that," and then, "Now."

When we finished my legs were numb. I sat down on the floor with my back against the washing machine panting. She stood beside me leaning her folded arms on the top of the washing machine, her head resting on her folded arms. After a pause she switched on her device and checked her readings. "We're just within parameters." She smiled. "Good work. We've made a great start. Now I've got to get going." She walked to the stairs. Without stopping she said, "I'll bring down your clothes."

She returned dressed and holding my clothes under her arm. I hadn't moved from in front of the washing machine. She set the clothes on the floor beside me and tousseled my hair playfully. "Not as easy as it looks?" When I smiled weakly she said, "You'll get the hang of it. And we have a lot more to do." She brought out an appointment book. "I'll be back on Thursday. I'll meet you here at two." She scribbled saying, "Please call if you can't be here. And don't worry, I'll let myself out."

When finally I heard the front door close I began to dress. By the time Eleanor came home I had run another load of dishes and two loads of laundry and also had gone to the grocery store. I told her someone had been around to see about the break-down problem. I told her the representative had assured me everything would turn out.

Eleanor smiled. "I told you so. You just worry about everything just to worry. You like to worry." She sighed then as she handed me a pizza box. "Work was so crazy," she said. The box was still warm. I was grateful for that. I showered early, went to bed and slept dreamlessly.

Cathy arrived on Thursday carrying a new chart. When she'd laid it across the dining room table she said, "The house is now calmer and more open to your intentions. There is still a lot to do but energy is flowing, the organism is more relaxed. In no time this home will be purring in your lap."

I asked, "Where do we start?"

Studying the chart she said, "We'd better go back to the basement before we begin in the kitchen. After that, the stairway to the second floor. I'm getting resonant phase shift that's locking your house into a perpetual grumpiness. Gravity within this phase space extends a temporal echo which we do not feel as repetition, but the resonance in- phase is causing distortion from upper harmonic canceling. It's as if your house was half- asleep and determined not to wake up. We're dealing with this calmly. We don't want the house to become angry with you."

"No," I said, "that would be awful."

I followed her down into the basement. Before we finished she had said, "Again, harder," and, "To the left." Afterward she took measurements and checked the chart.

In the kitchen she embraced the refrigerator, said, "Now," and then later took measurements on the floor on her hands and knees.

On the stairway she held onto the handrail, and afterward took readings at both the top and the bottom of the stairs. When she had dressed she said, "Don't be discouraged, we're making progress."

Cathy returned to our house pathology sessions several times over about two weeks. Finally she seemed to be satisfied. "The relationship you share with this house is about to be transformed. The house has begun to like you. But we should be prepared for a relapse. Habits are hard to break, whether you're a human or a house. Eventually the house will lose patience with you. That's the moment we're waiting for. Remember my number and call me as soon as there's any sign of break-down."

When Eleanor came home that evening she prepared a wonderful pork loin and asparagus hollandaise. I told her I thought I had the objects and disasters issue finally and completely resolved. She smiled as she opened a charming chardonnay. Over coffee she invited me upstairs to bed. Before I went up I placed the dishes and soap carefully in the dishwasher, moved gently, and the dishwasher purred.

The house ran flawlessly for nearly three months, until one night in a rain storm the roof began to leak. I was watching our trash can roll into the street to be hit by a passing car when I heard dripping in the kitchen.

Cathy arrived panting. Her owl eyeglasses sparkled with rain, her eyes were large and hot. "We've got to get onto the roof!"

"It's raining," I said.

"That's why we've got to get up there," she said. "Conflicting energies are gathered just under your roof. They've created a point of transfer, concentrated all of the resources on that one point." She turned to me and smiled. "This is it!"

The rain fell lightly as we climbed to just below the peak of the roof. When we'd undressed she spread a blanket on the roof, the blanket became immediately wet. "That's all right," she said when I pointed this out, "I just hate what tar and rough surfaces do to my skin."

Sometimes she said, "Go!" and for a while she muttered, "There now there, there now there," and then she said, "Yes!"

The rain had all but stopped when we finished. We folded the wet blanket, made our way off the roof. In the kitchen she said, "Mind if I shower?" I said Eleanor was a very heavy sleeper so I thought it would be okay. Minutes later Cathy appeared dressed and towel-drying her hair. She smiled beautifully. She said, "So it ends!"

I said, "What?"

"Gradually the cascade of sub-atomic structures merging and breaking off draws off all residual energy concentrates in temporal tide pools on the edges of phase space. A general purge results in the reformulation of structures. Eventually the concentration moves to the point farthest from the gravitational center of the structure. We had to be there at that moment. We had to be there to disrupt the resonance pattern once and for all." She kissed my cheek. As she left, over her shoulder she said, "My bill will be in the mail."

The next evening after dinner I told Eleanor I had finally taken care of the problem. She smiled, she seemed genuinely relieved. We made love under the dining room table with the lights turned on. And nothing broke down. For months on end things have run perfectly. Those months have become years.

Shamelessly I have begun to neglect everything. I abuse appliances, mis-apply their finely segregated designs, I torment orderly storage. I pummel the appropriate operation and maintenance of every manipulable system. I have thrown out all the instruction manuals. Efficiency has lost its charm. Things must break down occasionally. I have thumbed Cathy's business card to near-obscurity. I walk past public phones and mutter her number. A crisis is demanded. A break-down fulfills the metaphor for my discontent, source and explanation for all which focuses my unhappiness. Women metaphorize organically; our house is a mischievous but adorable puppy. Mechanical metaphorizing is favored among men, the finely geared clockwork, the gears invisible but interlocking. A metaphor must count for something. Sub-atomic physics and phase-space and fluid dynamics and quantum electro-dynamics. A metaphor ought to count for something. Meanwhile, my clockwork must fall apart. Gravanometric readings would undoubtedly indicate that the pull in the fabric of time has widened, things refuse their ordained places. Eleanor is always very tired at the end of the evening, she fails to notice and these metaphors just don't excite her. I sit beside her as she sleeps and watch our clockwork gradually unwind while the evening breeze billows the curtain beside her pillow.

I understand that it is sometimes the case that the cure is worse than the disease.

THE PAST IS AN OPEN BOOK

IN THE CHECK-OUT line at the supermarket Carolyn realized that at home she had left all of the electric lights on, the gas ranges burning and oven lighted, and the water taps open in the bathroom, in the kitchen and even in the laundry room. She was not certain why she had done all of this but she had no evidence to contradict its realization. The poverty of her best recollection initiated her curiosity. With two large bags of groceries she walked to the curb and flagged a cab in the hope that her home remained, wherever it was.

The driver loaded her bags into the trunk as she told him her address. He hesitated. Returned to his driver's seat he spoke at the rear-view mirror. "You want 1927 Walnut Street."

"No, I'm certain that I want to go to 2113 Panama Street."

"Unfortunately, passion and conviction are not truth. If you want to go to your home, that's 1927 Walnut."

"I remember clearly that I live on Panama Street, and I want to be driven there now."

"We'll pass a hospital on the way. I should take you there instead. Maybe you bumped yourself on your head. And then you might sue me or something. That sort of thing happens more often than you think."

"I never bump my head when I go shopping."

"Everything explains something," the driver said into the rear-view mirror, "but nothing explains everything. The worst of it is how far apart our lives have moved. I was, after all, your substitute history teacher one day in junior high school. I remember that day so well because I had been, I thought, rather more clever and even a bit saucy, what with the discussion of the Hanseatic League and the Council of Trent."

"Now that I hear the words Hanseatic League, I feel a sudden warmth flow through my body. I blush. Perhaps I remember you better than I'm prepared to acknowledge."

"Breathlessly I've followed your life in the newspapers. There was the explosion and fire at your hillside home, the demonic repossession of your car, the airplane crash of which you were the only survivor, the cat eating the dog, the miraculous credit card."

Carolyn shuddered and sighed. "I only remember the sense of invasion, the fear of nullity, the hallucination of highlight. But long ago I accepted responsibility for the collapse of the French franc and that remarkable disaster in the shoelace market."

"Your life has inspired a Hollywood encomium, preparations have begun, sexual scandal and corporate chicanery blossom like mushrooms after the rain. I do not wish to embarrass you, but the path of your exploits has left many of us nauseous with pleasure. Perhaps our marriage was wrong for people our age, but we were ardent and well- equipped sexually."

Carolyn gnawed at the corner of her handkerchief. "The times in the photo-booth at Woolworth's," she said, "and how we writhed about each other, our skin slick and hot. In the basement at Strawbridge's, and on the second floor by the science books at the Book Trader, and in the school yard at the Greenfield school on Chestnut. Our bodies entwined in a cramp of pleasure." She smiled. "It comes to me now. You tried to stop me. You discouraged the snake handler, wrestled the one-armed stevedore, insulted the sub-director, out-witted the doctoral candidate in philosophy. You tried to lead me along the enlightened path, the sunlight at the end of the shopping mall. How foolish I was. So blind yet so knowing, the doors swinging open and closed but then open again, as if opening and closing was sufficient. It all passed so quickly. What was there that didn't pass, hadn't passed, that would never pass again. It was the passing, after all, and not the being-passed, that so thrilled us then."

Finally the cab driver turned. "It would not be much, I admit, but we could try once more. Freed from the baggage that has accumulated between us, the lost years, the exhausted metaphors, the dismal afternoons anticipating nuclear holocaust or lottery success, we held hands in the dark and whispered with our eyes closed."

"But I once lived at 1927 Walnut Street and now I live at 2113 Panama Street. I should not trust you, you distort the truth."

"The truth cannot be distorted if it has come from the heart. The heart knows the truth as the horse knows the hay to make merry the way, whatever."

"Life at 2113 Panama Street has seemed so confining. There is an expectation of nothing, a degree of boundless air. I might already have lived there forever. It could possibly have happened and I have just now discovered it."

"And if you have escaped," the driver asked, "why would you go back?"

"How can one escape if one is not confined? If I am not confined, I can't escape. This seems obvious to me." The cab had been in motion some moments when she glanced up saying, "Drive me to the old place on Walnut Street."

He drove to 1927 Walnut Street. As she stepped from the cab she saw that all of the electric lights were burning, a stream of water flowed from under the front door and down the steps, and a plume of grey black smoke drifted over the roof of the house.

To the cab driver she was excessively grateful.

THE ABDUCTION OF AMANDA

HER STOMACH WAS FLAT as a book, her eyes were violet, her dark hair was thick and abundant and she wore it close to her face. And when she laughed mischievously she held the tip of her tongue between her teeth. This was my Amanda, my most recent true love.

After years of thick sobs and brooding over misplacement and self-doubt I decide she must be abducted. Held undoubtedly against her will in the cold dank castle by the neighboring count - a man of no little means and accomplishment - I would probably arrive just in time.

But first there must be preparations:

1 - acquire controlling interest in a glue factory.

2 - marry a prominent movie starlet

3 - engage in a scandalous affair with the inventor of the office memo

4 - renounce all ties with the local volunteer fire company

5 - lead an attack on a prominent governmental official, preferably the director of some department having little to do with children

6 - drive through the Lincoln Tunnel one hundred times

7 - divorce the movie starlet wife to the huzzah of major media representatives

8 - drive through the Holland Tunnel one hundred and fifty times

9 - become a prominent government official overseeing a department having little to do with children

10 - establish the first all-volunteer trash collection service

11 - denounce the inventor of the office memo as a servant of the devil

12 - sell the glue factory for an unconscionable profit

Our horses are less than the finest but ours is a lusty, intrepid band, dressed in a blaze of bright colors accompanied by intoxicated musicians working for below-union scale along with a representative of the Internal Revenue Service. We are prepared for many contingencies as we ride out into the bleak wind-swept parking lot of a now- abandoned commuter train station. As our journey progresses I inspire my followers with tales of Amanda's amazing hair, of her amazing eyes, of her amazing flat stomach. Sometimes I improvise conjectures about her firm slim thighs, the tiny dimple in her chin. A raucous chorus of cheers follows each of these revelations. We are lusty and hearty, our large white teeth flash in the moonlight.

Near dawn we stop at the 7-11 and drink coffee, a brightly festive crowd, disheveled and lusts only slightly slackened after an all-night march, gold and silver trimmings of our arraignment phosphorize in the bright sunlight. The horses discuss the situation nervously.

The manager's dog has only three legs. I ask if the dog can come along. The manager laughingly agrees saying it's about time he saw some other parts of the country. He slaps my back, laughingly spills my coffee. He reappears in an instant with another cup fresh from the pot, along with one for himself. We breathe the steam from our coffees grinning at the sun. The manager leads us all in a toast to lowered interest rates, job expansion, the end to dog license fees and the successful abduction of Amanda. The dog's name is Max.

As we ride and Max hobbles into the rising sun I sing new verses to the song of adoration of Amanda, my increasingly lusty band of eagle-hearted followers join in the chorus:

> You've been gone so long, Amanda
>
> Where did you go?
>
> What did you do?

We stop at an intersection, a funeral party of automobiles parades across our path. The leading hearse moves at a walking pace, the cars behind travel inches apart. My aide-de-camp speculates that the deceased could have been president had the winds of fate moved in another direction. I ask president of what. Max sidles up to a tall stately oak tree; with his missing rear limb he is perfectly equipped for sidling up to large stately oak trees. My aide-de-camp announces that stately oak trees are Max's métier. The sound of his urination angers certain members of the funeral party, they gesture furious behind automobile windows. My hearty fellows, however, cheer lustily.

A police car pulls up, a uniformed and armed officer exits and approaches. He asks, do you know how much prestige accrues from having a near-presidential funeral cortege pass through your city? He says, we in city government have angled and wheedled for this event for eighty-seven years. He continues that this is by any measure a major investment. But what I really want to know, he finally says, is what possible enchantment could set you and your lusty band of followers on this quest?

In reply I sing the first three verses of our homage to Amanda while my followers lustily belt out the refrains.

The police officer seems unconvinced. Then he notices that on my small finger I wear the amethyst and aluminum hexagon of the twelfth rank of St. Xerxes. Immediately he kneels in the dust of the street, places my hand on the bald spot at the top of his head, offers his glass and plastic octagonal of the twenty-eighth rank St. Xerxes. With subtle gestures of my hands and feet I indicate what needs to be done. He steps into the funeral cortege and halts its progress providing a gap between the automobiles.

We pass between the automobiles and resume our happy parade, their occupants de-car and applaud loudly. As the drunken musicians stagger and wave, hands are laid on auto horns in a triumphant cacophony. The cheers become deafening when the representative of the Internal Revenue Service passes through. Max sidles up to the tire of the nearest funeral car, hysteria spreads through the crowd. Indiscriminate hugging and embracing begins. Someone removes the coffin from the hearse, its lid is removed and the coffin is propped on edge in the middle of the street. The funeral flowers are strewn hither and yon. Laughter fills the air. I am tempted to join the general embrace and good cheer, my lusty band can hardly be restrained. But to the cry of "Amanda, On To Amanda", our line reforms, the musicians drunkenly re-group, Max takes his station by my side. With a last hearty cheer we resume our journey refreshed by the popular support we have gathered.

Our entourage stops at the local Safeway for a resupply of provisions. I dole out the stipend for provisions in pennies. Each of my hearty band must have: two cans of sardines, a box of Triscuits, five boxes of Pom-Poms, one Chunky bar, three Mars bars, seven packages of crackers-and-cheese, six cans of green soda, one pomegranate, and a pack each of cigarettes - Marlboros for the men and Virginia Slims for the women. For Max there's a t-bone steak he's allowed to smell frequently.

At the check-out counter I peruse a tabloid and discover:

1 - the market for glue has gone through the roof and stock values have tripled

2 - my former-wife movie starlet is now the c.e.o. of an international chemical cartel

3 - the inventor of the office memo has retired to a nunnery and there prays for my soul every day

4 - rival volunteer trash collection groups have begun open warfare for the very best trash

5 - I've been stripped of my high government position since I've been late for work five times in a row

6 - the Lincoln and Holland tunnels have been connected forming a great u-turn beneath Manhattan

In the parking lot I gather my loyal and lusty supporters. I begin my Our-Bridges- Have-Been-Burned speech, the same I've delivered in a variety of situations for years. Max sidles up to my leg, I step away just in time and Max falls over.

I quote from a speech by Thucydides in the Attic Greek, a speech by Solon, another by Julius Caesar in Latin from the Gallic wars. My followers are moved. I remind them there is only one choice, the choice to continue on. A voice from the crowd asks since we have only one choice, can that legitimately be a choice. Several of the others who have lighted their cigarettes join in the dispute. Phenomenology is mentioned, relativist theories of various stripes are brought forward. A splinter group develops. I appear calm while panic gathers in my thighs and legs. But my followers rally as I add new verses to the hymn to Amanda. I even add a slightly changed refrain:

>	You've been gone so long, Amanda
>	What did you see?
>	Who did you screw?

The change in the refrain causes consternation in the ranks though the drunken musicians universally approve. The representative of the Internal Revenue Service is clearly of two minds. I refer the matter to my aide-de-camp. I say, is this my fatal blunder? He says, no, because you will prevail and abduct the raven-haired and dimpled- chinned Amanda, and that's all there is to that.

To the murmuring crowd of disenchanted supporters and traitorous thieves I announce that the refrain is hereby changed to have- sexual-intercourse-with.

This alternative is widely deplored. Finally I suggest that at the word you ******, anybody can say whatever they want to say, or say nothing, just sort of hum along and that's fine, that's okay. Eventually half the group says screw and the rest hum loudly.

We approach the castle wherein I believe Amanda is held captive at dawn, our lusts unslaked for days as we tremble at our loins. Even Max.

We hide in the bushes beside the castle's swimming pool until the count, egg be-smeared from his successful breakfast, climbs into his station-wagon which spews noxious vapors into the distance.

Suddenly it begins to rain. Some are for taking cabs home. The best remain with me including the drunken musicians who haven't been paid yet along with the representative of the Internal Revenue Service who doesn't have cab fare home.

We hurry to the back porch and cluster under the awning. I knock. The horses grazing beside the swimming pool discuss matters in urgent whispers. I rap loudly on the screen-door. A woman opens. I am here, Amanda. We are here to abduct you, your abductors are at hand.

By god she says come on in I haven't been abducted in years and it's raining like crazy come on in before you catch cold my god how many of you are there come on in we'll go to the kitchen have some coffee I was thinking my being abducted days were about over but here you are let me take some coffee-cake out of the freezer take a few minutes to defrost in the oven.

Amanda, I've missed you.

Well I must admit it's about time you got here to abduct me I was beginning to wonder you had me guessing I thought maybe it was all just a gag.

I was a fool and I let you go.

My aide-de-camp motions me aside, brings to my attention the fact that her hair is neither abundant nor dark, her thighs are not slim, her eyes more grey than I'd led him to expect. He notes there are in fact few resemblances to the Amanda of story and song. And besides, the musicians want to be paid now.

I usher the leader of the musicians into the living room. The ceiling is twenty feet up and the room extends at least forty feet in any direction. He and I sit in chairs close together. He looks to the ceiling and claps his hands to check the echo. I tell him there's plenty of room, all the room in creation, more than enough room for musicians to practice. I promise him that he and his group can play here every weekend for scale. When he hesitates I add that there'll be free beer for the band. He agrees instantly, but then becomes downcast, says he is sorry never to have met the Amanda of story and song.

We return to the kitchen. The entire group is laughing outrageously as Amanda sits near the center, the tip of her tongue held between her teeth. The enchantment is complete. I tell Amanda to get her coat, it's time to be abducted. She smiles and throws her arms around me. Her stomach is no longer flat as a book.

Just then, the count bursts through the door. Having suspected all along that just such an abduction might take place he has secretly returned. He asks three or four impertinent questions concerning the over-all theory of abduction before I can assure him that there is no danger, I am simply here to abduct Amanda.

Amanda begins making pancakes, members of the abduction team assist, soon there are stacks of pancakes everywhere. We eat a lot of pancakes. As we finish the last of the pancakes the count turns to me saying, I will let you be count and abduct what's her name over there if you like but only on one condition: that you let me have this lusty band of abductors. He admits that just lately he's been thinking there's someone he had better abduct before it's too late.

When I communicate this to my aide-de-camp he demands the count stand and name the subject of his abduction. Misty-eyed the count says Beatrice and begins the song of the broad-bosomed and beguiling Beatrice of beauteous aspect, bountiful and well-shaped, of long straight blonde hair. Either her, he says, or maybe instead how about the unearthly Vivian, thick hair wavy and red the color of autumn leaves, shimmering gold eyes, broad shouldered, fine chinned and fine nosed.

Indecision begets a rift in our lusty band of abductors. The count sings both hymns as I hold hands with Amanda. We all join in the refrains. Finally it is put to a vote. Vivian the Vivacious is chosen unanimously, even some of the drunken musicians sign up for her abduction. The count, momentarily down-cast perhaps with regret that Beatrice was not chosen, manages to smile flattered by our intrepid band's enthusiasm. Amanda curtsies one last time, the count graciously hands me his crown and eggbeater, reminds me of the eggs that will come to me.

With a final rousing chorus of the hymn to Amanda the count and his band of lusty abductors file out the kitchen door, lusts yet unslaked. After long deliberation the horses have gone, but have left a line of cabs at the curb. The ex-count hands around piles of money from large pockets. Some of the musicians pile into his station-wagon. Amanda and I stand in the driveway waving spattered by the rain as the caravan drives away. Max sidles up to Amanda, she fails to move. The representative of the Internal Revenue Service takes a suite of rooms in the west wing of the castle where he pays rent and helps us dodge taxes. The rest of the musicians become drunk and agree to stay on for a while, but later that agreement evaporates when I lower their salary and cut off the beer allotment. Several eventually will take useful jobs as public accountants; despite what you've heard, musicians make very good accountants. Amanda considers removing another of Max's limbs but the geometry never quite works out.

On the back porch on a warm evening with a stack of pancakes by my side and Amanda roasting asparagus over an open fire to be spread with cheez-whiz and eaten hot, and with our continually drunken musicians tuning in the distance, I become nostalgic for the days of abduction, the heady euphoria of the chase and the camaraderie of the fiery abductors. But when the sun has finally set and the darkness of the starlight is complete, Amanda's hair is almost abundant and almost dark, her eyes are almost violet, her thighs are almost slim and her stomach is almost as flat as a book. And the tip of her tongue flashes between white teeth when she laughs.

WITH A BLUE-BLACK MANTLE, twilight covers the material world along with Bruce as he walks to his car. Visible in the shadows a man studies that car; Bruce spots him almost immediately and watches him. Dressed in tatters and rags, even in the muddy weak light it's obvious the scared, pasty skin of this man's face has not seen a razor for days. A homeless, useless bum, Bruce decides, and he does not like him. Bruce does not feel intimated by the man, he is not afraid of him, but he finds the man furiously annoying. So instead of continuing to his car, Bruce turns and walks toward the man, wondering just who the hell this guy thinks he is. It occurs to him this man might be working for Gloria. The surmise leaves him pinched between amusement and fear, and Bruce finds both emotions stimulating. He keeps his car keys in his left pants pocket and his money in his right; he is determined to avoid surprises.

Bruce walks deliberately toward the man, waiting for him to realize he has been discovered and then slink away. But this man does neither. Bruce reaches mid-distance but the man remains quite still. Bruce slows and begins to wonder. Like everyone else, Bruce knows that small armies of crazy people walk the streets without restraint. Craziness is not something Bruce thinks much about. He knows it exists, like a sixth finger or worms in the blood, but he has no curiosity beyond that. His approach to the man slows, the urgency of his indignation fades. He studies the man's eyes. He has been told that this is how one can judge whether a person is crazy.

So he approaches the man watching the man's eyes and not his own feet. And when he steps into a crack in the concrete he falls very hard to his knees. This fall startles Bruce, but his eyes never leave the man. Face utterly immobile, an expression of indifferent curiosity, the man simply watches Bruce fall as he might watch a leaf blown by the wind.

Bruce recovers awkwardly brushing at his pants but in a moment he is standing again. His knees are raw and sore, pant legs torn open. But he does not even glance down to inspect the damage. He stands still and waits.

To Bruce it seems a very long time until the man speaks. "Hurt," the man announces. It is not a question but a statement. The softness of his voice surprises Bruce, and he realizes he anticipated something harder and more angry. Mismatched shirt and trousers, worn and dirty and too light-weight for the season, beaten and dusty canvas shoes. He is a heavy man of medium height whose face holds the thickened blur of alcohol. Yet his voice is smooth and pitched higher than his years. When he speaks the man's expression does not change.

"I'll be all right," Bruce says. Glancing down he brushes at some dirt on his torn pants, then inspects his scuffed shoes certain he is about to get to the bottom of all this. "You're following me, aren't you?"

To Bruce's surprise the man's expression does not change. But the man hesitates. Something moves about his lips and a glitter appears in his eyes as if a flicker of thought has brightened in his mind. "Indignant jamboree kerosene."

Bruce pauses, certain he has misunderstood. He steps forward as if distance is a contributing factor. "Did you just say something?"

"Limpet manifold nectar. Orbital pectoral quiver radiation stratification, totemic undercarriage validation winding xylem yogurt zephyr."

Bruce waits longer this time before he attempts to think. He has heard distinct syllables which sound entirely in English. But he does not understand, so he waits. Bruce recognizes these as the dark times, days when fog is so dense, vision so obscured that only with some assistance can the path be recognized. So it occurs to him that he needs to understand what he has just heard, if only to decide if he needs it at all. He admits that the sense of those words has eluded him. It occurs to him that his fall, though not injuring his head, may have provided such a shock to his body that his thinking could have become disrupted. He decides he must repeat his question. "I want to know if you are following me. Yes or no."

A sparkle of recognition in the man's eyes, an instant as if illuminated, his lips curl and ripple as he says, "Aurora Bethlehem. Corvette. Deltoid elegiac fumble."

Bruce's patience does not drain away slowly, it vanishes. "Look," he says taking another step forward, "you better stop screwing around. I know you're following me. Don't fuck around; just tell me what this is about."

"Globe hemorrhoid, igneous jansanary kilim." The man speaks with a hardly perceptible movement of his lips, as if he is muttering quiet secrets with an old friend. Goaded by the man's tranquility, tantalized by a suggestion of interior motionlessness provoked by the off-handed cryptic, Bruce is suddenly furious.

"Go back to Gloria and tell her if she thinks she's getting any more of my money she'll have to do better than you. Understand? Just make sure that message gets back to her." He takes a step forward toward the man. When he takes another step Bruce realizes what he is about to do. Yet it's as if what is about to happen is not actually happening but only appears to happen. As if right up to the last moment he will discover himself elsewhere in the midst of something else. So he does not hesitate to take another step.

The man's eyes do not grow large, his lips do not suddenly curl with anger, his chin does not suddenly jut forward nor do his nostrils flare. Instead, he speaks very quickly. "Lectern mistletoe napalm. Orangutan pedophile quotation resplendent. Statistic terraform ulterior victimize. Wavelength xercon yeoman Zimbabwe argonaut. Blasphemy cuttlefish duplicitous entrapment flotilla."

In a moment Bruce realizes his face is wet, discovers tears in his own eyes. He realizes that as he listened to the man he has begun to weep. Bruce wipes his face dry with the palm of his hand. He cannot account for his growing sense of betrayal and fear. He becomes furious. Hands clenched into fists slowly rise as he leans forward about to take another step. And the man speaks again.

"Gullible harmonium identical jukebox kryptonite. Labdanum misanthrope nematode oxymoron Pleiades. Quantum redolent sycamore. Tourniquet umbilical vagrant warden vedic warp xylophone. Yeast zenophobe aggregate. Ballast comatose divide elevator flamingo gluttony haberdasher."

"Okay, so you're from Gloria." Certainty comes to Bruce in a moment.

Suddenly he is calm, his hands relax and his arms fall to his sides. He is not yet ready to smile, but everything else in his mind has vanished, a vista of blue-grey opens before him. He mocks himself, chides himself that he should have picked up on this from the start. He is, he thinks, smart enough at least for this. After all, who else would care where he has parked, or when? Even the tone of the man's voice provides evidence; it's as if this man intentionally imitates Gloria's soft high-pitched voice.

Yet the man's face remains frozen, motionless but not serene, nor content, a fine mesh of tension enwrap the muscles of his face so that his eyes seem to peer through a mask. "Irrigate jumble kite," he says, "label motor notation obelisk precipitate. Quail robust statutory tailgunner umbrella vinegar. Waffle xerophyte yellow zoomorph antler. Beacon callous derrick exile. Facility granite herbarium ignition juridical."

And then Bruce begins to smile.

Finally he enjoys a sense of completion. A sense that after all there is some purpose, some overriding principle at work in this universe. And finally he recognizes his connection to it. It all has come to him in a flash. His understanding is as sudden and clear as daylight; he realizes that he has just been told Gloria's business partner is a man named Derrick, that he is a lawyer for a well-known insurance company, and that the two of them have a plan for Bruce.

Bruce is utterly certain the man has told him all of this, in so many words. This man has given him the information he needs to save himself. He resists the temptation to embrace him. But his relief turns back to concern when he detects no change in the man's expression, even while he has recognized these explosive revelations. "So tell me what else you know about Gloria's plans?"

The man's face remains still, but subtly at first his lips begin to move, even before he begins to speak, as if he is very carefully arranging the sequence of his words, their purpose, position and cadence, their specific function and relevance.

"Kindred latent mutable negotiate occupation peripheral. Quartet relational sequential. Tangential ubiquitous vertical window. Xenia yardage zinc astronaut."

The pieces of the puzzle snap into place. Now Bruce understands that Gloria and Derrick have a third partner, and the three of them plan to take over his company. So this surveillance, like their divorce, is part of a larger strategy. Bruce feels a wave of gratitude toward this man. At serious risk to himself, he has told Bruce what he needs to know. And Bruce is relieved. At least now he knows where he stands. But he also knows he is in a tight spot and out-numbered. He can do what he needs himself, but he likes his chances better with some help. "How about you come work for me? What do you say?"

"Bucolic cataract deviation." The man's expression remains impassive, and Bruce becomes worried.

"But why not? I'll pay you better than she does."

The man does not hesitate, as if already knowing his response. "Elevation franchise grotesque helmet intravenous jocular."

Bruce is surprised. He has not anticipated such loyalty. He knows well that Gloria can be very persuasive, particularly when she deploys her sexual advantage. And Bruce's ex-wife has a lot of ammunition. Combined with deep-pocket partners, the cards are all stacked at Gloria's end of the table. Bruce can hardly blame this man, destitute and confused as he is. But he realizes the man represents her only hope.

"All right, how's this? You help me save my business and I'll make you a full partner. How does that sound?"

The man's expression changes very gradually. His face relaxes slowly, tension around his eyes and mouth drains away. And then behind his eyes a light appears. For a moment something flickers across his face that might be a smile. But the concern in his expression has not entirely gone away. The man's lips again begin to move before he speaks. "Kelp leucocyte maintenance neologism oscillate perjury. Quiver rotate syntactical trilobite ulterior vermillion wavering."

Bruce believes himself a good negotiator, always capable of coming to agreement with anyone over anything. Except of course Gloria. But his best offer has just been refused. What he needs now more than anything is a stall, a way to temporize. Bruce needs time to get an angle on this one. He needs to know what this guy wants most. And he needs sufficient time to do it. So he says, "Tell me what she's paying you and I'll double it."

And Bruce gets what he wants. The man looks hard at Bruce, a look on his face as if he might be hard at work thinking. Thinking for this man seems to be an unusual excursion into unfamiliar territory. Although the man stands quite still, to Bruce he appears to be running very hard. Eventually almost breathless the man says, "Xenolith yacht zombie. Apex bolt cardigan denture epaulette. Finial gaseous hardware irrigation. Joint kapok leaflet millimeter nutritious."

Startled, Bruce wonders if Gloria has grown generous in her old age. Of course, for Gloria to make this man such an offer proves she's desperate. So Bruce wonders about Gloria's partners, and whether her partnership is entirely voluntary.

The grey of fading evening removes the last blur of light. Bruce concludes that if this is her best ally, Gloria is in deep trouble and she knows it. And if she isn't frightened, she should be.

Bruce shakes his head. "That's a hell of an offer. Gloria herself can't have that kind of money just lying around, but I'll bet you know where it's coming from. Don't you?"

The man's blood-shot brown eyes blink hard twice, his lips move but make no sound. Bruce waits knowing now that he knows all this man knows. "You're her last hope, aren't you?"

The man stands very still and does not blink. Bruce can't help but smile. "Those other two have her by the short-hairs, but you're going to get her off the hook. What I haven't figured out yet is how. So why don't you fill that part in?"

The man's eyes widen. The change in his expression so startles Bruce he feels for his coat pocket. The man's eyes go to Bruce's hand. He takes a step back. "Odiferious perpendicular quagmire rustification solenoid. Tempestuous ulceration vertical wainscoting. Xenogamy yataghan ziggurat albino. Balustrade comforting denizen elongate fistula. Gargle herringbone iodine jugular krimmler lanolin mortice nasturtium."

Bruce recognizes the panic in the man's voice; the man now understands what's about to happen. And this makes Bruce feel better. And Bruce wants to be certain the man understands. Smiling, he says, "You never were very good at picking friends, were you?" The man says nothing, only glances from Bruce's eyes to the hand in his pocket. He does not move.

"As far as business partners go, you've got the worst luck of anybody I ever met. And maybe that's what it all comes down to. Just dumb luck." Bruce understands that Gloria's last hope stands before him; get him out of the way and Gloria's partners do to her what Bruce should have done to her a long time ago. Thinking this, Bruce's smile widens. Not because he likes what he is about to do, only for the result. As Bruce's hand moves toward his waist the man's eyes grow larger.

"Oscillate peculiar quotidian," the man says. He begins to tremble. "Resign stalactite treasury unilateral vengeance willow xeroderma yawl zealot albacore beetle. Carboniferous ducal endgame facilitate gambol." His hands fly about his ragged and torn clothing, his lips move.

Suddenly something appears in the man's right hand that surprises Bruce. The sight makes him stop and freeze in place. "Well," Bruce says as his smile fades, "after all is said and done, I guess Gloria hasn't done all that bad for herself after all."

Slowly, smoothly, evenly, the man aims the dull-silver revolver in his hand at Bruce. Bruce does not hear the shot that pierces his chest killing him in an instant. Nor does anyone else; the silencer works perfectly, the gunshot hardly louder than a burp. Just as smoothly as he brought it out, the man slides the gun back into his clothes. He looks down at Bruce and mutters the word, "Hurt" as though he has just invented it. He turns then and walks slowly away, murmuring and murmuring a string of words which appears to have no significance.

CANTALOUPE: THE FRUIT OF FRIENDSHIP

I AM TOLD THE CANTALOUPE is a sacred fruit, best enjoyed sun-warmed and nearly over-ripe, when the pale orange juice runs down your chin and over your fingers and down your arms. Split open it reveals a primordial world of orange with white seeds enmeshed in a glistening soup nestled in a small cavern at the heart of the fruit. Such a food is the sweetness of life itself.

My failure is that I don't really like cantaloupes. A small failure I believe and, despite Catherine's objections, not unreasonable nor my worst. But the juice becomes sticky and I can't quite wipe it from my fingers no matter how many napkins I use, until I'm forced to leave the table and wash up. And leaving the table I also leave my wife Catherine and my friend Barry to sit together at the table alone while I'm upstairs washing up and drying and then come downstairs to find Catherine and Barry have changed seats and they smile to each other. But this has nothing to do with the sacerdotal nature of cantaloupe. Human weakness cannot constrain divinity.

Barry bellows his enthusiasm over the quality of my cantaloupes as he licks the pale orange juice from each of his fingers. Catherine giggles without comment watching Barry's fingers enter his mouth one at a time to be loudly sucked. Her eyes dart from him to me in a child-like secrecy. Catherine has never before struck me as the giggling type.

I've never been of the suspicious type, unfortunately; unfortunate because suspicion is the mother of all knowledge and only the stupid are not suspicious. They never ask enough questions when they ask them at all, while not asking questions advances no one's knowledge. So by not asking what they are smiling about, even after Barry has gone home and Catherine and I are stacking dishes beside the sink, my knowledge is not advanced. Nor is it advanced when I don't ask questions later as we're sitting together to watch a show on television about the destruction of the rain-forests of Brazil with the concomitant demise of small odd-looking animals. Nor is knowledge advanced when I do not ask questions as we undress and go to bed, nor when in a drowsy coma Catherine invites me to make love to her.

Those cantaloupes I planted in the spring have grown substantially after the recent rains. Recalling his enthusiasm for them I call Barry inviting him to stop by and take a few home. He laughs quite pleased saying he would love to but asks if he can stop over the next day. The next day is Saturday and would be fine except that due to another crisis at my office I've planned to put in a full day's work. And I confess a fear that the cantaloupes will be over-ripe by then and may even have begun to rot. But Barry assures me he likes them very wet and juicy so he isn't concerned.

The cantaloupe is an oddly beautiful fruit. A grainy, almost rough, surface when fully matured, they appear nearly spherical and achieve appropriate size to bring to mind the eggs of beings fallen from space and determined to conquer the earth. Knock lightly on a fresh one and listen; that's the sound you want, that's how you know.

I return home from my Saturday's work to find Barry sitting on the couch in our living room watching television just as Catherine descends the stairs wearing a bathrobe and toweling her hair dry. Barry stands saying he'd only arrived a few minutes before and that he knew I'd be home soon, so he decided to wait for me. Catherine comes to plant a kiss lightly on my cheek while asking how the day's work went and was it awful. The television is tuned to a children's cartoon show and Barry turns suddenly toward the screen as he begins to laugh. He pretends he loves Bugs Bunny as a way to disguise his embarrassment although I suspect his statement might be true. Meanwhile, Catherine disappears into the kitchen so I offer to accompany Barry to our backyard garden to choose his cantaloupes.

I admit that my annoyance when I reach the garden in Barry's company is unjust since this is my garden after all, even if Catherine has promised to take some responsibility for its maintenance. Weeds have propagated enthusiastically after all the rain, and I mentioned something to that effect to Catherine as I was leaving that morning. She volunteered to get at the weeding before I returned from work, and appeared to take some pride in that. As far as I can now make out, however, she weeded a small patch beside the cantaloupes but that was all. I stand over the pile of pulled weeds lying beside work gloves and kneeling pad all appearing abandoned as if by surprise. Catherine is never careless with gardening tools but that does not strike me as out of place. I've purchased a number of implements for the garden and Catherine is correct when she points out that several duplicate the uses of others. Fair enough, but those duplicates also reduce the number of tools needed to perform certain gardening tasks. Besides, she isn't obligated to use all of them at once. I've explained this to Catherine and she seems to have perceived the logic. But this discouraging jumble of rakes, shovels and shears of various sizes and hues does tick me off. Barry ignores my pique and rhapsodizes over how successful our garden is this year. And I can only agree; the fruits and vegetables have grown almost as quickly as the weeds around them.

Our patch of cantaloupes really does resemble a group of unearthly eggs laid in a wild green nest and I must admit they are tempting. Barry kneels to praise these cantaloupes and suddenly his enthusiasm is unrestrained as he taps each lightly and declares it the model of perfection. I am overwhelmed with pride. What he says is true; these cantaloupes are prize-winners and in response to his praise I'm eager to cut one open. I stand to one side enjoying this up- welling of pleasure. Grinning with pride I glance back at the house. Catherine is standing at the large second-floor window watching us, and she is bare-chested. Catherine is not remarkably shy but a public display of herself like this seems out of character. She sees me looking at her but she hesitates a very long moment before she smiles and then steps out of view.

When I turn back, Barry is still studying the cantaloupes murmuring words of praise of their size and shape. He asks if he can hold them, and I can only oblige, he is enjoying himself thoroughly. I then suggest he choose the two he likes best. Meanwhile I know that Catherine will begin preparing dinner soon and so I invite Barry to join us for dinner. But he refuses saying he's already enjoyed enough of our hospitality and the gift of the cantaloupes will send him on his way.

Secretly I am relieved he has decided to leave since I have become tired of the hyperbole he enlists in praise of the cantaloupes. With his two cantaloupes in hand we return through the house where we encounter Catherine. She is now wearing a rather revealing light blue cotton dress. She steps over to Barry and kisses him quickly on the lips saying she'll see him soon. She then disappears back into the kitchen.

Barry stands with a cantaloupe in each hand watching her go and he mutters, you're a lucky man, although I am no longer quite certain which of us he referred to.

Several nights later our phone rings and Catherine picks it up. After some quiet talk and odd moments of low laughter she hangs up. It is Barry, she says, and he's completely out of cantaloupes so she's volunteered to drive over and drop a pair off for him. I have planned to watch the evening business report on television so I tell her that yes, of course she should go, but to let me help her pick out the best.

The night sky has become almost dark and insects and children can be heard all around us in a low cacophony. I hold the flashlight and Catherine follows. We arrive at the patch and immediately I spot one of the two to send with Catherine. She stands to one side watching me step carefully among the vines. As I pass the first back to her I'm momentarily distracted by the color of the sky and the first stars shimmering against the blue-black velvet.

I turn then to watch Catherine bring the cantaloupe to her nose to breathe in its aroma, and then she does an odd thing; she kisses the rough pale brown and green skin. She does not see me watch her.

I search the patch for another but none of those left are of quite the quality of the first. Still, I want Barry to have two fresh cantaloupes so I pluck the one closest in maturity and sweetness and pass it to Catherine. She holds the first between her feet as she takes the second. After holding it a moment she sets it on the ground beside the first and asks for the flashlight. In a moment she recognizes the marginal inferiority of the second and she insists she will not make this journey with an inferior cantaloupe. She turns and abandons the second nestled in the thick wet grass.

I'm compelled to applaud Catherine's remarkably well-trained eye, a result no doubt of our three-year union, so that what she was not born with she has acquired. The cultivation of such careful discernment allows her to recognize quality along with that dedication which would not allow an inferior gift to be passed on to a friend.

I fall asleep in the living room chair waiting for her return, awake abruptly around three-thirty in the morning when she lets herself in at the back door. She disguises any surprise at seeing me and throws her arms around my shoulders apologizing for having kept me up so late. She says that as she was leaving Barry's she discovered one of her tires had gone flat. He invited her to wait inside his apartment while he called a garage, except they both had a few drinks while waiting and then fell asleep and hadn't awakened until only an hour before. She acknowledges it was all ridiculous and embarrassing but she decided not to call me because she assumed I was already asleep.

I stand and stretch and discover that I'm sore at every spot in contact with the partly-cushioned chair, but also relieved finally to see her and to have her arms around me, and I easily imagine all of the evening's events happening just as she has described.

I draw her close and notice her hair smells sweet and her cheek and throat smell of cantaloupe. There is a dreamy quality to her smile as she leans into my arms. We stand together and I walk beside her up the stairs to our bed and brief but furious love.

Days later another early evening phone call which Catherine answers. After a brief muttered conversation she announces that Barry is expecting dinner guests any minute and has decided that our cantaloupes with vanilla ice cream and perhaps brandy would provide the perfect last act for the dinner he's preparing. Catherine assures me that she'll reach Barry's, drop off the cantaloupes and return within an hour. The fact that Barry hopes to impress his dinner guests with two of our cantaloupes flatters me enormously. And while I regret that I can't leave the house having planned for an early meeting the next day, Catherine seems eager to do so, even suggesting she might have one drink there before she starts home. Perhaps it's my expression, but instantly she smiles promising she won't accept any drinks and she'll be home within the hour.

I volunteer to go with her out to the garden to help pick the cantaloupe for Barry but Catherine smiles stepping past me saying she's already chosen the ones she will deliver. She kisses my cheek and goes out the back door toward the garden. I return to the living room where the reports I'm working on are spread over the couch while the tv plays a show about continental drift and offers images of the sequence of glacial ages which I find fascinating. Moments later I hear Catherine's footsteps in the gravel beside the front drive. I step to the front window and lift the curtain. She reaches for the car door with her hands empty. I drop the curtain, listen as her car door latch clicks open. The door closes and in moments she drives off.

I take the flashlight into the garden and look. I need only a glance to realize none of the cantaloupes have been removed from the patch. As I feared, she has somehow forgotten to take the cantaloupes with her. Immediately I choose two wonderful examples I'd been saving for an up-coming visit from Catherine's parents, toss them into a plastic bag and get into my car. I'm confident that if I hurry I can arrive soon after Catherine does and thus save her the embarrassment of appearing without her cantaloupes.

When I arrive I see Catherine's car parked and that I'm too late. Bag of cantaloupes in hand I walk to Barry's apartment building's door. Moments after I press his buzzer his voice comes over the intercom asking who it is. I announce myself and ask that he forgive Catherine for having failed to bring her cantaloupes, but that I've brought them with me and I'm eager to come up. After a long pause he tells me that actually he had decided that he and his guests would enjoy some honey-dew melon instead, and Catherine had generously stopped at a local fruit stand and with her remarkable good taste had chosen two sweet yet firm melons which he and his guests were now enjoying. He's certain that because of this they couldn't do justice to the marvelous cantaloupes he knows I've brought.

I then ask to speak with Catherine. There's a long pause after which Barry describes how much he admires my hard work in the field of raising cantaloupes and that there isn't another like me within a hundred miles. This of course is a terrible exaggeration since I know several talented amateurs in the area. But I can only be flattered by his praise and I tell him so. I then ask to speak with Catherine. After another long pause he says that it appears she's gone to the bathroom but that he will invite her to call me at home as soon as she is free.

I remind him that I'm still holding two cantaloupes for his guests and I'd be happy to walk them up to his apartment if he would simply buzz me in. I assure him it would be a shame to waste such beauties now that they've been picked. Again there's a long pause before Barry apologizes that at the moment he can't leave his guests nor can he allow me to come up, so that with the greatest unhappiness he assures me he'll be in touch soon and that I should be careful driving home.

After a moment I buzz again, and again Barry's voice comes over the

intercom. I ask if I now can speak with Catherine. Another long pause and
Barry says that as far as he can tell she is still using the bathroom but that he
will remind her to call me the moment she can. He wishes me good night and
I wish him one in return.

I hesitate, momentarily frozen, the cantaloupes in the bag hang at the end of
my arm a terrible weight, and then I ring his buzzer again. It takes a long time for
him to answer this time, but his voice pierces the darkness almost visibly through
the intercom and asks what it is he can say to convince me to give up my vigil
on his doorstep. I remind him of the cantaloupes in my bag and their sweetness
surpassing perfection waiting to be carved tenderly and handled carefully
preparing to nibble and bite and suck. And then I ask him when it all changed?
When did cantaloupe fall from its pre-eminence among fruit and concede the
leading place to the syrupy and cloying honey-dew melon?

His silence is maddening and I buzz twice when it continues too long but
finally he admits he doesn't know, but that he treasures his experiences with
the cantaloupe along with the vistas and horizons which have opened for him
as a result of my suggestion that he familiarize himself with that wonderful
fruit. He adds that the memories he shares of our adventures with cantaloupe
will remain with him forever and forever sweet, and that this sweetness he has
shared would remain part of him. He then thanks me for all I have given him.
He leaves me little to say except to ask one last time to speak to Catherine.
After another long pause Barry says that Catherine says she cannot thank
me enough for having introduced the two of them to each other and that she
knows that all I want is for her to be happy and that whatever makes her happy
will make me happy so that I should be happy now that she is happy. Wishing
me good night again he reminds me that Catherine will call me soon. With
everyone now happy there seems nothing left for me to do except leave with
my happiness and my cantaloupes, which I do.

The change of season has begun in the garden. The days are still very warm
but the evenings are becoming cooler. As I work there I see the brown of the
new season appearing cautiously everywhere. Soon only the pumpkins, now
just beginning to take shape, will give any indication of the delicious harvest
I've gathered this year. Recently I received a letter from Catherine. She is in
Spain with Barry and her letter is filled with delightful descriptions of the
various melons she has encountered there. She writes that she will send seeds
for my garden and that she hopes they will grow and yield satisfying fruit. I

have heard nothing from her since that letter, but there is always tomorrow. In the meantime, after the first frost I'll clear the dying plants and prepare the ground for winter. After that it will be time to go through the catalogues, comparing the various breeds, looking for something new perhaps.

133

INVISIBLE PLEASURES

I VISIT THE ADMIRAL.

We sit in his living room. The Admiral's trailer has no air conditioning; we sit across from each other in a sweating contest. I want to borrow money and he knows it. He takes off his blue and white sports shirt, waves it to fan the thick air.

The Admiral served with distinction. The recipient of many medals of commendation, he wears them pinned directly to his skin. His chest, his arms, his legs, even some on his back, he puts them everywhere, pinned beside the wounds he's suffered to get them. One pinned to his right side just below his breast is so heavy the skin below it forms a fold. Beside some of the medals there are thin trails of blood. He catches me staring. Disguised behind his mirror aviator sunglasses he grins.

"Like that one? Battle of Constantinople. Saber thrust knocked me flat on my back. Gutted the bastard anyway. Hell of a day." He drinks from the glass of bourbon held in the hand not waving the shirt. He's told me about this one before. As if he can hear me thinking he says, "Nobody talks about it any more. As if those brave men weren't dead." He's said that before, too.

"This one here?" He points to a long, vicious scar across his stomach. He's told me about this one, too, but I say nothing. "Battle of Leponto. Seen eight out of every ten of my crew die that day. Cannonball set off a powder magazine not as far from me as you are. Dumb luck I only got this belly cut. When I come to half my intestine laid on the deck beside me and everybody within twenty feet of me is dead." He puts his glass down on the floor, picks up the bottle and refills my glass. He always tells it the same. Exactly. When it half-fills he puts down the bottle and takes up his glass again.

"But you want to take a look at this one." He points to a scar on his side about an inch across and perfectly round but depressed deep into his skin. Beside it hangs a large gold star enameled in bright red. I know this one, too. "Piece of shrapnel big as a coffee- can lid punched through my rib-cage, shaved my lung, and lodged half way out my back." He turns slightly, the exit scar is a narrow jagged line. I have sometimes seen it in my sleep. "Just enough stuck out to nail me to a wood bulkhead. Like you might pin a bug to the wall, I couldn't move. Battle of Bengal Bay." His grin seems more menacing. "You think this weather is hot." He leans forward and refills his glass.

"What happened?" I ask. I still want to borrow that money.

He shrugs. "A light cruiser rammed us port side. Ship heaved, I heaved with it, the metal stayed stuck in the wall. Like having your spinal cord ripped out of your back." From a box on the table by his hand he brings out a cigar. "Good men died that day, too."

The Admiral offers one to me but, as usual, I decline. He takes his time lighting it, watches closely as the flame licks the blunt end. As if he is no longer thinking of anything except that one point of shimmering light. Something keeps me from corrupting his silence. And he knows this. His tales are a foreign language wedded to a cacophonic music.

"See this one?" He jets a plume of blue smoke through pursed lips as he points to his right upper arm. The medal beside it is shaped like a golden bird with blue and turquoise head and wings, maybe two inches across. I've always wanted to own that one.

The scar below it has the rough, irregular outline of a tree-branch. All around it is obvious burn-scar tissue. "Battle of Petite-Dejune; the Tasmanian Armada in '23. Torpedo. I was below-decks with a fire team. The explosion sent a piece of one of the trucks we were transporting flying. The metal was so hot, the cut was seared shut as soon as it was made. The cut was nothing but the burn took months to heal." He grins, tugs on the metal, blood flows brightly.

Finally I say, "See that?" I point to my right eye. "I was eleven years old." The scar is faint and covered by my eyebrow, but I insist it's there. "Five of us having a stone-fight. I ducked behind my best friend, trying to use him as a

shield. The stone caught me across the eye." I smile. "Or how about this one?"
I hold up my right hand, extend my index finger. On the inside is a small deep
scare shaped like a V. "Got this while I was living in southern France. Got
drunk with a woman one night, the bottle slipped off the table between us, I
reached to catch it before it broke. Missed. Didn't matter, though, we were both
drunk enough by then." I lean back, and suddenly I'm no longer sweating.

The Admiral's grimace twists his lips. "The scars of pleasure are invisible."

Then he leans to one side and reaches into his pocket.

HERE COMES MR. AMMANOGATZ.

Mr. Ammanogatz has a theory, and he has come to the Mall today to test it.
He's worked on this theory for years, the calculations have been most complex.
But the implications are astonishing.

Mr. Ammanogatz passes through the huge glass doors that give him
entrance into the Mall. He has passed through this portal countless times,
and has consistently encountered the same phenomenon. A few steps past
the threshold, his entire head is suddenly gripped with a mild but insistent
pressure. Not quite a headache; just pressure seems to originate behind his eyes,
spread subtly over the frontal lobes of his brain, and then behind his ears in the
form of a heat, and finally gathers as a knot at the base of his skull. Despite his
discomfort he smiles with relief. Everything is working as his theory predicts.
He begins to stroll.

As the second postulate of his theory—called the Ammanogatz
Theory—predicts, as he walks along the broad indoor avenue, the pressure
and configuration of his skull—discomfort varies according to the different
merchandise of the shops he passes. Thus, he finds the pressure strongest
passing the sex-toys shops, the auto-parts shop, the book store, the liquor
emporium, the record shop. Less severe pressure results from walking by the
men's clothing stores, jewelry and china shops, garden supply shops, drapery
and furniture shops. He receives no stimulation as he passes shops selling
baby clothes, sofa art, gift cards for all occasions, and women's shoes. His
experiment proceeds.

As the third postulate predicts, each time he reaches a severe pressure point,
the act of passing through the doors and into the offending shop relieves the
pressure instantly. But upon leaving, as the third postulate also predicts, unless
he has made a purchase the pressure returns. Today, as he walks toward his

rendezvous, Mr. Ammanogatz is finding confirming evidence for each of his postulates. The notes and charts of wave fluctuations and irregular patterns he has drawn over the years have taken him to this meeting with Mrs. Bernoulli, and the Final Experiment.

Mr. Ammanogatz enters the pharmaceutical mini-store and observes the throb within his skull intensify, the frequency of alterations increase. He walks to the back of the store, a corner wall of brightly colored boxes of toothpastes and toothbrushes in plastic cases. When he sees her dark green coat and dull grey hair, her back is turned toward him. Mrs. Bernoulli has been a reliable collaborator in a lonely field of research. As he approaches, almost as if she senses his presence, she turns. Her blue eyes are limpid with love. They stand close together in the sight of only one security camera.

Mrs. Bernoulli leans toward him, places her hand lightly on his forearm and speaks quietly. "I don't know that I can go through with this." Mr. Ammanogatz realizes she is trembling. "I am beginning to feel foolish."

Mr. Ammanogatz is startled.

"There must be some other way," she continues, "to demonstrate this theory. Something less violent, less confrontational. Or at least less dangerous." Though her voice is insistent she speaks so quietly Mr. Ammanogatz must lean forward to hear.

But Mr. Ammanogatz has already considered this objection, and has already formulated a response. He tells it to her and she says, "Oh well, okay. If this will benefit science."

"You have what we need?"

Mrs. Bernoulli nods. From the orange plastic shopping basket on her arm she hands him a small brown paper bag. Without opening the bag he feels along its contours. He whispers, "And all of this is worth at least ten dollars?"

Mrs. Bernoulli's bright blue eyes widen. "That is a fundamental parameter for the experiment. And I have gathered the articles from each of the twelve aisles, just as you outlined."

Mr. Ammanogatz smiles, gratified that the control of this experiment will be so precise. Finally he will thoroughly prove something. He takes the bag from Mrs. Bernoulli's hand and slips it into his pocket and the pressure on his brain changes into a pulsating massage. As he feels himself turn to look at the check-out register he says, "And you're certain none of these have been paid-for?"

Again Mrs. Bernoulli nods. "It is time," he says. His feet turn in the direction of the register. Mrs. Bernoulli watches him closely. "Take our purchases up to the register," he says solemnly, "and I will pass behind you." The waves begin to intensify, Mr. Ammanogatz feels himself gliding uncontrollably toward the orgasm of a successful purchase.

Along parallel aisles both advance toward the register. Mr. Ammanogatz is giddy, suppresses a chuckle, recognizes Mrs. Bernoulli as an attractive woman. Just as they reach the register, Mr. Ammanogatz falls a step behind Mrs. Bernoulli. He watches the movement of her hips, pulsating waves of pressure pause between momentary tremors of delight.

Mrs. Bernoulli slows and then stops at the check out. Mr. Ammanogatz is nearly ecstatic with pleasure. He slides behind her as she stops to pay for her purchase. His deception is successful, the clerk does not notice he is about to leave without paying for his products.

As Mr Ammanogatz reaches the door that will return him to the Mall, the sudden rush of pressure in his skull is so fierce he is certain he has been hit at the back of his head by something very hard.

He turns and watches Mrs. Bernoulli complete her transaction. Then he watches her approach. To his dismay, Mr. Ammanogatz staggers. He is certain the person behind the register is carefully not looking at him. The pressure behind his eyes has turned the world another color. He is no longer certain where the floor begins and ends. He knows he cannot long withstand this torment. But he has planned for this possibility as well. He returns to the register, brings out the products, offers them to the clerk's inspection.

When the clerk completes the transaction Mr. Ammanogatz feels a sudden rush of elation, a feeling of being cleansed. A feeling of celebration. Mrs. Bernoulli steps beside him, looks up deeply into his eyes. "Are you all right?"

"All right?" Mr. Ammanogatz smiles. His skin smells of his satisfaction. "Better than that." He grins and stares deeply into Mrs. Bernoulli's eyes. "I am correct!" He wraps his arm around her waist, draws her to him. She does not resist and leans toward him as though she thinks not at all of Mr. Bernoulli.

AT THE EMERGENCY ROOM I SUFFER ALIEN POSSESSION. The duty nurse points me to a line of plastic chairs against the wall saying that someone will be around to see me. There are wires and cords attached to the chairs and no one else is sitting there. The wires are red and yellow and green and blue and black and other colors, and some of them are thicker than my arm. Tiny purple sparks come out the ends. I ask if I should take my clothes off, but the nurse is already talking to another nurse. I tell her the pain is getting worse. She has red hair and she does not turn to look at me. I go to the chairs. My thoughts lead me to search for the exit, but the chairs invite me to try them. So I do, although nothing seems to become better.

I look and look, and then I see him walking toward me. He is a dark angel with biceps as big as my waist and the pecs of a god. His dark hair curls across his forehead. He smiles as he sits down; he doesn't seem to mind the wires. He grins as he asks, what seems to be the matter?

"I am in pain," I say. His warm full lips purse in sympathy. What sort of pain, he asks.

I study him carefully. And then I see it; the perfectly spherical ball-joint at his elbow. I am relieved. "You're one of us, aren't you?"

This devil-man turns to look around. No one is near us. "Of course," he says. "I know just how you feel." And then I see it. It's as though I'm looking at his x-ray image. His entire skeletal structure has been replaced with tungsten-carbide rods, and high-tension cables encased within latex sacks have replaced his muscles. Behind his eyes I can see the micro-chip circuits that connect him to the mother-ship. He is utterly beautiful.

He leans close to me, a perfume I don't recognize rises faintly from his throat. He whispers in my ear, "Believe me, we should consider ourselves fortunate. Look around you; all of this misery. Bodies breaking, falling apart, misshapen and corrupted, doomed to dissolution amid sheiks of torment. So much pain, it is too terrible even to watch. But look at us." His eyes are green, they glow suddenly bright. "We have received a special gift. What we see around us is not our fate, and we know this."

His perfume dulls my senses, my body seems to go slack, I lose my strength.

"There," he says, "you see? Remember what it was like before?" His hand is perfectly shaped, the musculature is subtle, its strength sheathed in elegantly molded pseudo-flesh. He lets it rest lightly on mine. It warms against my own, the perfume becomes more powerful. "Pain is more difficult to recall than pleasure, but not impossible."

Even as his hand lays on mine I recognize the subtle glow of the polymer base of my own new flesh. I confess, "The tiny motors and pumps and the warmly humming circuitry inside my chest still bother me. I feel a great loss.

I have been emptied and not completely re-filled. I have yet to rejoice in the promise of my bright future." His green eyes stare deeply into mine. "I want to go back."

His smile becomes sympathetic. "No you don't. You only think you do now. You sentimentalize your corruptibility. As though illness and death were like bike-riding, something you once enjoyed, as best as you can recall." He leans close nearly whispering in my ear. "The mother-ship needs us here to observe. In exchange for this service we receive her remarkable gifts."

And he is right, I now have the best body I have ever had. But the grinding of the metal, the buzz of electricity, switching circuits snapping on and going off, all of it has destroyed my sleep. "This body will not adjust to me."

He smirks amused. "But you do not need to sleep. At least not very much."

I am shocked. "How did you know I was thinking about sleep?"

Again he shrugs. "You know my thoughts as well." Suddenly I realize he is right; I begin having his thoughts along with him. It's sort of like dream-dancing, and I'm getting good at it. "Sleep as little as you like," he thinks. "There are so many other things you can be doing." The image of two people having sex occurs to us. We grin. "Yes, of course," he says, "that, too."

Suddenly I feel much better. "And all I have to do," I ask, "is wait for the mother-ship?"

He shrugs again. "Pretty much. From time to time you'll receive a special assignment. But don't worry, the mother-ship will simply activate your mind control. You won't know a thing about it, but whatever purpose they need your body for will get done."

The wires at my feet and around the chairs suddenly seem docile. Even the purple sparks sputtering from the ends seem friendly, almost musical, like water rushing through a stream. He pats my shoulder lightly. "See, I told you everything was all right."

And he's right, the pain disappears, I feel perfect.

MY BODY, MY PLANET

"THIS MUST STOP!"

That was how Doctor Sagan talked to me while I was still on earth, and before I got stuck drifting around in outer space. She was a nice lady but she went to school too long. And because she stayed awake and believed what she was told, she thought she knew something. Schools have the unfortunate effect of convincing people of their own reality while denying every other. I hated contradicting her, and happily she didn't think I was stupid. I smiled and nodded at her words and then returned her serious look. "Size," I said, "is power."

She rolled her eyes and sighed.

I said, "Throughout this universe there is a direct ratio of size to power." Hearing this she tossed her pen onto a little white metal table by the wall. She watched me hop off the examining table. Hey, who am I kidding? It took half a minute for me to shift my weight from my ass to my feet. I said, "Just think about Jupiter," because I felt terrific.

She said, "You know what I'm going to say."

I shrugged and then nodded because our exchanges had come to this. She had nice eyes; the kind you would want someone who was mad at you to have, the kind that say I'm mad at you, but if you smile, in another minute I won't be. I didn't tell her that it was all and only about Carol. Our exchanges lacked candor while dissemblance reigned. So instead, I smiled.

"Gravity," I said, "is the inverse ratio of mass to distance."

She was unimpressed by this news, but I believe it's the only thing we ever need to know. That's what it means to be universal. It also gave me something to say while I got back into my clothes. Which took a while. Shoes had become the toughest; by twisting and bending I could just tie their laces. Watching me struggle, Doctor Sagan said, "You should buy yourself loafers."

Red-faced and breathless from leaning over, I grinned. "And give up the lightheaded excitement of my sense of myself as an object dominating a universe of smaller objects as the ultimate submission to materiality? I'd have to be nuts." I straightened my tie, adjusted the shoulders of my sports coat, and prepared to re-enter the community of much smaller persons.

With a careful pat on her shoulder I said, "You're a type of scientist and therefore know less than you believe. For this reason you'll dismiss my claim that the force I emanate is drawing my living room furniture toward me. As I've grown larger, it's all moved closer."

Doctor Sagan yawned. "Does this have anything to do with alien abductions? Because if it doesn't, I have other patients."

"In just the past year," I said because I hoped to appeal to her scientist's enchantment with numbers and its suggestion of skepticism, "that furniture has moved nearly three inches. Think about that, Doctor; matter is attracting matter. This can't be disputed. Your Isaac Newton proved that, as those objects draw closer to my chair, they accelerate. So as I become larger, that attraction increases. You may not be charmed by this idea but by this we both know that eventually my furniture will crush me into a pulp."

"Funny, I've never had a patient defend obesity quite that way." Dr. Sagan was charming even when she was annoyed.

"Increasing mass," I continued, "will add to that internal pressure eventually generating temperatures which will ignite a nuclear fusion reaction, just like our friend the Sun. Think about that. My fusion-reactor living room will provide cheap electricity and without pollution." I laughed as derisively as I could. "And you insist I'm too fat."

She shook her head with annoyance. "Imagine that; personal physician to a nuclear-fusion reactor. Could I get any luckier?"

"Write a book," I said. "Go on tv. Become an expert in something. Finally become somebody other people want to talk to. What's to complain?" I tried to look hurt.

She was not impressed. Rolling her eyes again she brought a business card from the pocket of her jacket. "Don't come back until you've talked to this woman." Her wonderful grey-green eyes glittered with passion. "You show up here with anything less than a bad case of death and she tells me she hasn't talked to you, you'll have to stroke where you stand to keep me from throwing you out." I took the card hoping her smile would reappear, but it didn't.

There was nothing more to say and I didn't say it. I struggled through the door ducking down when I had to. Not only had I gotten wider, I'd become taller. Which was just as well as even Doctor Sagan agreed, if I expected to get bigger. I navigated a corridor wide enough to allow three people to pass. But my explanation had failed. Nothing would convince her that big was good and that the larger I became the more power I'd accumulate.

She followed me along the corridor until we reached the reception desk. I took her hand. Nearly lost in mine, it felt like a kitten's paw. I said, "We'll see each other again but under better circumstances. Meanwhile, take excellent care of yourself, and I promise I'll do the same."

She pressed her hand against mine as she looked up into my eyes. Something seemed to pass over her eyes that I might almost misunderstand as love.

I maneuvered through the front door and out into the parking lot. The step-van with my couch in the back started, my company's driver waved as he backed to the curb. I stooped low, grabbed the strap overhead and lowered myself into the couch. Two taps with my foot on the floor and we were on our way home.

Carol always understood what I was accomplishing, and how far I might still go.

"I told you she wouldn't understand." Carol spoke as I struggled through our front door. Fortunately we have always lived in houses with high ceilings and wide doors. "Professionals are invariably baffled by the obvious." Carol is the smartest person I've ever met, and that's saved us whenever our situation demanded it.

Carol and I married young and when I was still small and thin. I'd started with the Company as a messenger boy, and from that position I saw the most stupid decisions I could imagine. It took a decade, but my bulk increased with my power until I became the largest and therefore most powerful man in the most powerful company in the most powerful industry in the most powerful country in the world. Pretty good for a skinny, high-school dropout.

Carol's petite body perched like a sparrow on the edge of our swimming pool- sized, reinforced bed. She took a portion of my finger in what she could of both of her hands, smiled, and squeezed until I felt her caress.

"I have good news," she announced. "The contractor's promised to have the garage fixed up by next week." Assuming we were about to run out of room, we decided to remodel our four-car garage into living space. Carol had drawn up the plans, but because of all the reinforcement the garage demanded, several contractors had turned us down. So her announcement was a great relief. Once again, and as always, I was in her debt. She is a sweetheart like they don't make anymore, and this world is poorer for that.

When we met, Carol recognized my potential as well as my problem. She saw what no one else did; that I was a person who'd accomplish something, and thereby take up a lot of space in this world. And she reminded me that she'd married me because she'd understood me.

For me, it had been love at first sight. I found myself so happy in her company that I had no ambition to change. And at first she seemed satisfied, always affectionate and encouraging. But her encouragement was subtle, and so she allowed me to believe that I came to certain conclusions entirely on my own.

We'd been married nearly a year when finally we confronted the fact that, despite my experience I had never received an increase in responsibility or salary. So when I decided I needed to do something about this, she was ready with a plan.

Carol enjoyed sharing this news about our garage. Her own employment is in public accountancy, but as an extremely smart person, her occupation is merely that hobby which brings her a reliable salary. And because she is so adept, I have left it to her to negotiate with contractors. She took pleasure in this and why not; she is undoubtedly smarter than anyone she has ever talked to, an advantage in any negotiation. As a result, the walls of the garage would be extended and reinforced, and heavy timbers would form our new bed. I am grateful to Carol, and I have tried to prove this every day.

Her plan for my self-improvement was surprisingly simple; I must become larger.

A small person herself, Carol recognizes the power of those she encounters who are large. But she understood that an element of such attraction is simple physics. It was up to me to take advantage of this most fundamental law of the universe. So she began to feed me.

Beginning with a single full grocery bag as a meal I was astonished that I grew quickly along a rising curve. The discipline, I'll admit, was terrible, and occasionally I slid back. But Carol was the soul of patience, resorting to ingenious encouragements. Her passion for my achievement was breathtaking, but it took a while before either of us noticed significant results.

At first I assumed it was my imagination, but strangers began to stop me on the street and ask what I thought. At first their questions were innocuous: what did I think of the local sports team, or the mayor's election, or a new tv program? But over time these questions moved to serious matters involving the Company. What did I think of this department or that manager; how did I think sales would go in the coming year; should we move the water cooler to the other side of the office? One day the president of the Company bumped into me passing in the hall, and invited me to have lunch with him. Finally I decided I was not dreaming.

When I described all this to Carol, she became so excited she cried. She coached me on what to say at our lunch, how to hold myself, when and how to embrace the president warmly.

Lunch was so successful that over coffee the president offered to resign and put the Company in my hands. "A big job," he said, "demands a big man." I could only smile and nod. He continued, "As the biggest man in the firm I was sure I was the only one worthy of this job. But your progress has astonished all of us. You're the big man now. Not only do we find ourselves increasingly attracted to you, we feel greater confidence in the power you project. In fact, among the smaller members of the company your attraction has become irresistible, another argument in your favor." All of this was just as Carol had predicted. So I was prepared.

I pretended to be surprised and flattered, and when finally I appeared compelled to agree, I reminded him I'd need his help during the transition and assured him I'd value his advice for a long time. This was all a lie, of course, but as Carol's suggested, with that lie I made a smaller man feel better while it cost me nothing. Lunch concluded, we stood. I was now several inches taller than he and nearly a hundred pounds heavier. I stepped toward him, but he rushed into my waiting arms, also just as Carol predicted. My embrace was as gently fraternal as I could manage. This was the beginning.

Carol had plotted a cunning strategy. From the first I attracted management talent to our Company, along with investment capital. Soon

I had attracted eight companies to request we buy them out. By the end of that first year our corporate assets had grown fivefold. And as I grew, the Company grew. Within two years I had attracted twenty percent of the total investment capital in the country. In our third year I had grown so large that our Company qualified for seats in both Houses of the Congress. At her inauguration ceremony the President became so strongly attracted to my upper right arm that Secret Service guards had to peel her from me. But there was no turning back, and I continued to grow.

Carol's enthusiasm for my achievement was easy to see. She enjoyed arriving at official functions sitting on my shoulder and wearing some particularly sexy gown. As a result of my bulk and Newton's law, she and I had become the center of a world.

This progress continued, and for that time I was satisfied. But every success eventually pales, each satisfaction inevitably fades, and every sweetness becomes bland.

I began to question the value of my choice, or the discipline it demanded, until I had to concede that my power was being wasted. All of that power demanded a greater object of attraction, something large enough to attract me and would make the rest of my species proud. This is why, when the President of the United States offered to resign if I would take over her job, I refused. My aim needed to be higher. Unhappily, my rejection of her offer made all the newspapers anyway, and her failure to attract me to that job cost her the next election.

Around this time and while we were still setting ourselves up in the garage, Doctor Sagan came to see me. She climbed over and around me as best she could, and I helped her whenever she asked. When finally she came to listen to my heart her eyes widened. Although her reaction pleased me, I waited. Finally she said, "This'll sound crazy, but I think your weight and size has increased so dramatically that you've grown an additional heart."

I could only smile. "Of course," I said. I already knew this and had only waited for her to notice; I'm not so big that I can't hear both hearts. "You're looking at the big two-hearted guy."

She scrutinized me with new respect, and even perhaps admiration. Or, dare I suggest it, a whisper of lust. Had I finally attracted even her? Still large-eyed with surprise she asked, "So what's next?"

This question pleased me since I'd been thinking it over. "This planet's become too small for me." Her eyes widened, as if she'd come to suspect the same conclusion a moment before I said it. "This bulk must have a higher purpose. Surely I can't exist just to attract more capital and increase shareholder value. There must be more to my life, this brief existence, than just making money."

Doctor Sagan smiled, the most thrilling I'd ever seen from her. She squeezed a portion of my arm until it tingled pleasantly. She said, "Your extra heart has expanded your soul." But then a look near anguish swept over her face. "So you're about to go where the rest of us can't follow. You'll go with our warmest wishes, but you'll go alone." I nodded sadly because I had come to understand this as well. "So we must say goodbye." She leaned as close as she could and kissed me somewhere on my cheek. "My heart goes with you." She hopped down from my chest, turned abruptly and her heels clicked away; that was the saddest sound I'd ever heard.

Over the several weeks after my visit from Dr. Sagan, and with Carol's help, I negotiated with the UN and the IMF until I'd brought about total world peace and eternal economic security. But my growth continued and so quickly that I was soon forced to move out of the tent we'd setup in our backyard. The Mayor invited us to erect a much grander tent in the City's largest park, promising us complete privacy. Unfortunately, by the time I engineered a worldwide ecological rebalance, even our City's park could no longer accommodate us. The new President offered a federal park for our residence in any state of my choosing so that I could continue my benevolent projects. Instead, I agreed to a temporary site in a nearby suburb. Regrettably, in the President's enthusiasm, a long-established community was leveled to accommodate me and my retinue. Events were moving beyond even my ability to direct. In public I disguised my intentions, but I'd already reached a conclusion.

Since the moment I first saw her, Carol had been all the world to me, and so much more. She had not made me what I'd become, but she'd encouraged and sustained my evolution. And even more, she'd offered complete faith that my success was inevitable, and that I need only follow my own footsteps to reach it. So, late on the night before we were to leave the city and take up a suburban life, I took Carol carefully into the palm of my hand and began to whisper. Though she said nothing, the expression on her face filled with anguish. I explained my plan, emphasized its significance, how the benefit to humanity would be greater than anything I'd done so far. My plan was audacious and involved tremendous risks, and each step would demand enormous effort. I suppose in the end my torrent of words overwhelmed her. Or perhaps my aspiration was so abstract she lost interest. But in the end she understood, and her resistance drifted away.

"So this is good-by," she said without looking at me. And because I couldn't deny her words I said nothing. "When will you leave?"

"Two hours before sunrise. To make as little a fuss as possible."

"And will you keep in touch?" Her eyes could not meet mine.

"Where I'm going they won't have a post office." I wanted her to smile. A stupid thing to want considering everything, but I wanted it anyway. When finally she looked up, her eyes were glassy with tears. And so, I believe, were mine.

For the rest of the night we laid awake together in silence, I on my back and she in the center of my chest with one hand resting gently against my cheek, determined not to count the passing minutes. But eventually, inevitably, the hour arrived. As I looked at her knowing this would be our last moment together, I felt such longing and such profound grief that I was afraid I'd cry. And perhaps seeing my anguish, Carol forced herself finally to smile. She said, "Go ahead, make us proud, and we'll all read about you in the newspapers." And then there was no more to be said. With one finger I caressed her cheek while her tears began to fall. I crawled to the entrance of our tent and then stood. With one last glance back, I began to walk.

Although I'd become enormous and hard to miss, I also knew the deployment of the guards, and so I had no trouble slipping past unnoticed. In my mind I'd mapped a route that took me through the quietest neighborhoods of the city. For nearly two hours I walked undetected until a police helicopter spotted me. By then I was past Pittsburgh. At lunchtime I could see the skyline of Chicago. In twilight I passed St. Louis, and then in western Kansas lay down to sleep.

Before dawn I was up again, passing Boulder by midmorning. The mountains were tough, but things smoothed out when I reached Utah. Outside Salt Lake City I contacted the President, asked him to have an aircraft carrier ready in San Francisco Bay. Although I'd disguised my first intention, hasty phone calls followed. Eventually I was told that an aircraft carrier could not sail for the Bay area in time for my arrival, but another was already in San Diego and ready to go to sea. The detour was inconvenient, but there was no way around it. He promised that another carrier would join us at sea in two days. I wasn't happy with the new plan but there was no alternative.

Arizona at nightfall is gorgeous. I wanted to push on to reach San Diego by daybreak, but I'd forgotten about the Grand Canyon. In the darkness I stumbled and twisted my ankle caving part of it in. My ankle hurt like anything, but I was really upset at having damaged part of such a beautiful sight. So, overnight and as my ankle healed, I did my best to fix those parts that were most disturbed. I hung around for a while after sunrise, just to make sure it looked okay and I must have made enough repairs because no one has ever suspected it looked different. But pride in my handiwork is misplaced since the Grand Canyon wouldn't have needed to be fixed if I'd watched where I was going.

I reached San Diego around noon. On the flight deck of the USS MasterCard I curled up for a snooze. The admiral already knew our destination. With the evening tide we cast off.

It was a good thing the President arranged a rendezvous with another carrier. Three days out I'd grown so much that my feet trailed over the back-edge of the flight deck. By lashing the two aircraft carriers together, I could at least get a good night's sleep. But that meant we couldn't travel at night, and this made speed even more urgent.

Passing through the Straits of Timor I'd become so large I straddled both carriers like a toddler on a tricycle. But there was so much drag from my legs that the engines could make little progress. So, much to the terror of the admiral, I paddled with my legs those last five hundred miles into the Bay of Bengal until we reached the mouth of the Ganges.

While we were still well out to sea I volunteered to walk the last few miles. To the commander and his crew I offered my gratitude and best wishes. They seemed as relieved to see me go as I was to get going.

Although the people of Bangladesh knew I was coming, and many had already seen me on television, the crowd at the harbor still became hysterical at my arrival.

After I'd apologized to the people of Bangladesh, I reached the foothills of the Himalaya mountain range just north of Decca and followed that toward the northwest. In daylight I avoided stepping on farmhouses, but during the moonless night farm families along the mountain range built fires in their rice-paddies which kept me on my path with the river as a glistening silver line to my left. I walked the entire following day without stopping for rest. Then, just before sunset, on the horizon glimmered the snow-shrouded pinnacle of Mt.

Everest. I lay down in a broad valley nearby, my first solid rest in days.

Again I was on the move early, and by sunrise I could see the Himalayas plainly along with the peak of Mt. Everest.

But it wasn't until late in the afternoon that I reached that mountain's base.

According to my plan the next day would be busy, so in the shadow of the highest spot on this planet's surface I cleared a snowfield for my last night on earth.

Yet I couldn't sleep. I was excited and worried, but what kept me awake were recollections of those I was about to leave behind. Because, even though I'd come a very long way, until now there had still been a chance to change my mind and return to Carol and Doctor Sagan. Towering above me, Everest's pyramidal peak stood sharply outlined by that sea of stars which sparkled around it. In its shadow I couldn't resist the flood of memories of cherished embraces. So, surrounded by ice and snow, I dozed in a melancholic and anguished reverie.

But finally, the eastern sky became pale, starlight weakened, those celestial fires receded and sunrise approached. After a brief glance back I began to climb.

I reached the summit just as the rim of the sun peered above the horizon and the faint crescent moon was directly overhead. With a foot planted on each side of the peak, I realized that my own height now reached nearly a mile. Yet I felt myself continuing to grow and at an accelerating rate though I hadn't eaten for days. Finally there was nothing left to do. My preparations were complete and I had reached my point of departure.

I took great deep breathes in rapid succession, filling my chest as I bent and flexed my knees. When the rising sun flashed into view, with an effort that strained every fiber of my enormous body, I leapt up, arms extended, fingers reaching, clutching for that nearly invisible moon. I closed my eyes and held my breath.

For a long time, the cold wind whipped at my face and sang in my ears as I felt my body soar. Then gradually I began to slow down. When I opened my eyes the curvature of the earth was like looking down onto a dinner plate. The Himalaya mountain range appeared as irregular lumps of sugar far below my feet, and at the horizon I saw both edges of the subcontinent with slivers of that turquoise ocean beyond. But soon, gravity would begin to take over until I reached maximum distance from the earth. Then, whether or not I continued was entirely a matter of Newton's physics.

But Newton was with me. Just as I felt myself begin to drift, a subtle force began to pull me in the opposite direction; I'd begun to fall toward the moon.

Until that moment, the plan I had described to Carol had been theoretical at most. But having become captured by the gravity of the moon, it was only a matter of time before I'd put the rest of my plan into effect. Newton is never wrong, and the speed of my drift toward the moon began to increase.

Though my lungs were still full of air, I no longer needed to breathe. I suppose that my body had begun to recycle carbon dioxide into oxygen and carbon all by itself. So my body already contained all of the oxygen I'd ever need since none of it would ever be consumed completely. Still, a tricky moment was near.

As I approached the moon I leaned into a path that avoided crashing into its surface and that led to a slingshot effect that would send me at terrific speed deep into the solar system. But this demanded exquisite timing. When I reached the correct point of entry, I exhaled all the breath still in my lungs. This burst put me on a tangent to the moon's orbit, and then the fun began.

I came around the back of the moon so fast I just about threw up. That would have been pretty nasty in outer space. But wow, did I have fun. In a few seconds I had passed the moon and watched it begin to shrink. Beyond it, earth looked like a sad blue ball.

Ahead I recognized the planet Mars; I was on target. But it hung there red and very small and I still had a long trip. So I made myself as comfortable in outer space as I could. I even took a nap, and maybe that's where my problem began.

I'd lost a bit of speed breaking away from the moon's gravity, but I was still doing a good clip. Yet I can only conclude that when I finally passed Mars and approached the asteroids I wasn't going quite fast enough. I'd planned to avoid contact with any of them but assumption is the mother of fuck-up; I was only half right. Which, in outer space, is the same as being entirely wrong.

What Carol and I hadn't calculated was the gravitational power that the mass of my body would have gained by then. How this could have happened I can't say. Carol is so smart it still seems an impossible mistake. But maybe tiny mistakes are the ultimate punishment for hubris, as well as my assumption that Carol would be perfect in every phase of my plan.

By this time my body had grown to more than two miles in length and probably a mile across although I was still able to maneuver between the larger asteroids. What I hadn't counted on were those smaller ones that began drifting toward me. Gradually these started to stick, slowly adding to my total mass. As that mass increased, larger ones began to drift closer. And as they got closer, their mass began to attract ones from farther away, and those attracted larger ones even closer. Of course, all of this was as predictable as an apple falling from a tree. But worse still, this increasing mass began to deflect my trajectory. Before I could reach the other side of the asteroid belt, I was wearing one. So Newton wins again.

Eventually I decided that Jupiter had become stationary, and I was no longer getting closer. I'd become trapped in a solar orbit along the path of the asteroids, and nothing short of universal annihilation could change that.

In the distance I can still just make out the blue speck of your earth, while more and more asteroids gather around me. Isaac Newton is after me and with a vengeance.

Wandering among these asteroids I've become a celestial vacuum cleaner. Those immediately around me draw closer, gravity increases with mass bringing asteroids further away under my influence. All those gathering around me clustered closer and tighter. Wedged into the center of billions of tons of rock, eventually my body will be crushed. This is a possibility I'd considered while on earth but I still don't think I'll like it much.

And that's the reason I'm writing all this down. When I've finished I'll tie this with one of my shoelaces around a small asteroid and hurl it back toward the earth, another reason it's a good thing I never followed Dr. Sagan's advice and bought loafers.

In any case, I haven't been gone so long I can't hit a planet with a rock. And if you're reading this, my aim must still be pretty good.

But I'm writing this for Carol. I want her to know I'm not disappointed. I won't be going to Jupiter like I had planned, and I won't be coming back, like we had hoped. I'm sorry I can't be with her, and maybe now I'm supposed to admit that, yes, this was really a pretty stupid idea. But like most stupid ideas, it wouldn't have been a stupid idea if it had worked. Still, at least technically, it was pretty stupid. So I'm counting on you to let her know that as far as I'm concerned, everything turned out okay. And while you're at it, I'd be grateful if you looked in on her, just to make sure everything is okay with her, too.

I guess that request is sort of lame seeing as how it was my decision to end up this far from her. But out here, cold and alone and knowing I'm never coming back, I still hope she's doing okay. I just want to let her know I miss her. But I also want to remind her that eventually, Isaac Newton will give her something back.

Eventually, after the asteroids around me have clobbered me into little pieces, we'll all be clumped together into a new planet. This little planet will just keep rolling around the asteroid belt picking up a pebble here and a boulder there. And eventually this planet of me will become full-grown. And that's the other reason I'm writing this. I want everybody to know that when I become a full-grown planet, I want to be known as the Planet Joe. Joe is the name of my favorite uncle, the nicest, smartest, funniest guy in the world. If I have to be a planet, which it looks like I can't avoid, I want to be called the Planet Joe, after him. This way, him and me will be part of the solar system together forever.

Anyway, that's what I want, and if you could do something about all that, you'll have earned the eternal gratitude of an entire planet.

THE PARK OF NO RETURN

ONCE AGAIN it's a different park today, and this is why Peter likes it.

The caretakers who lay out the Park each day scatter its benches like fallen leaves, one here, another there, and with several clustered together. But in the dead of night those same caretakers return and re-lay the paths. Some days, some benches are connected to each other, while others sit like remote islands in their trimmed green ocean of lawn. On other days, other benches are connected, and previously connected benches are cast adrift. For this reason Peter can be certain that every visit to the Park will bring a new adventure. Because Peter is an adventurer, he makes certain he pays the Park a visit every day.

One day Peter entered the Park, and immediately encountered a large, blue dog with yellow and orange patches on his chest and back. To the dog, Peter said, "You must be new to the neighborhood."

"Just moved down from Boston." The dog sniffed Peter's crotch, Peter stepped back too late. "My owner has a job at the University. I wish she'd left me in Boston, but you know how women are."

"No, actually, I don't know," Peter said. "How are they?"

"Oh, they're okay one at a time. But get them in a group and there's always trouble."

Peter nodded. He wasn't entirely convinced but he didn't want to appear rude. "Serious?"

The blue dog shook his head. "The worst," he said. "See, the university job is just a cover. My owner actually works for some secret intelligence organization. So secret she won't even tell me about it. Imagine that. Me, her own goddam dog. Who the hell does she think I'm gonna tell?" The dog leaned down and licked its crotch. "But I'll tell you this much. She gets together with her secret agent girlfriends and don't kid yourself, the bunch of them get into some stuff that would even embarrass a dog."

"Wow," Peter said, his mind chasing fantasies. "So how do you know all this?"

"You know how it is," the blue dog said, dejected. "They get a few drinks in them and they forget there's a dog in the room."

Having felt that way himself in the company of women, Peter could only nod in sympathy. "So these women are all spies?" Peter asked hoping to resurrect the conversation.

"They call themselves intelligence officers these days, though there ain't that much intelligence to share, if you get my meaning. But the pay must be pretty good."

"Not a bright bunch?"

"I'm just glad I can take care of myself. As long as my owner keeps her job, I'll keep eating. As for her girlfriends, well, they must have something going for them I don't know about."

"Still," Peter added because the conversation had almost become interesting, "being part of a nest of spies must be pretty exciting."

The blue dog shrugged his shoulders. "They sit behind computers way too much. But reality never got in the way of a good story. Am I right?"

"You couldn't be righter," Peter said.

"Like a couple of nights ago, they're sprawled all over the furniture in their lacy, black underwear nursing cocktails and trading stories about the Cold War, not one of them old enough to have been there. Telling stories they've heard, none of them with a story to tell of her own."

"Kind of like the rest of us," Peter said. "It's always more fun to tell a story you've heard."

"How does it feel to be wrong?" The blue dog was no longer listening, distracted by three dogs across the park trying to hump a fourth. "Amateurs," the blue dog muttered. "If they're going to do it with people watching, at least they could show some class."

"What kind of spy stuff do these women talk about?"

"Pretty ordinary, what you'd expect. Who stabbed who, where the wiretaps are, who's in and who's out. Real exciting if you're standing by the water cooler being paid by the second."

"And you're not going to share any details?"

"Oh man," the blue dog said, sniffing the ground around his feet, "can't you throw a stick or something? Ask them yourself, they're sitting over there watching us."

Peter looked up feeling as if he'd been caught doing something nasty. "Where? Which way?"

"There!" the blue dog said without looking up. "See those two old ladies holding hands? To the right, three women sitting together."

Peter finally spotted three young women dressed conservatively yet very stylish.

"What's your owner's name?"

"They have names now?" the blue dog asked with mock surprise.

"Look," Peter said, "I need to confess that, really, you're only a means to an end. Absurd as it may sound, I'm more interested in your owner than I am in you."

"She's a lousy fuck," the blue dog said, "so unless there's something else, scratch her from the A-list."

"You dogs are pretty blunt."

"We don't live long enough for the niceties."

"Yeah, I suppose you're really on the clock."

"We all are, pal. I live one year for each of your seven. Seven years of sex, drugs and butt-smelling packed into twelve of your months. Some hear the ticking louder than others."

"I guess that's true. But if it is, tell me her name and I'll let you catch up on your butt-sniffing."

"Man, you humans are worse than dogs."

"Give with the name and I'll walk you back."

"How does that work for me?"

"Works for me."

The blue dog growled before he said, "The one in the center feeds me, her name is Jill. The redhead's Ann, Sue's the brunette. Now, there's a cat over there I need to chase."

"Whoa!" Peter said grabbing the blue dog's collar. "I have to drag you back and claim to have found you and then get myself thanked and introduced. Believe me, it's nothing personal."

"Slick," the blue dog said, "but easier said than done," and pulled sharply on the collar. But Peter had a firm grip and dragged the dog in the direction of the women.

"Hey!" he yelled toward the women. "This your dog?"

The women glanced at Peter, their heads huddled together. The blue dog tugged and pulled until, a few feet from the bench, he broke away.

"Good riddance," the dark-haired woman Peter decided was Sue said with a relieved sigh. "Dog talks too damn much." Peter decided she had a nice smile.

"Dead weight," red-haired Ann said. Her blue eyes were sharp and bright and seemed to mean something.

"That dog cost me good money," Jill said, annoyed about something. Her blond hair was cut short, her nose was small and pointed.

"Sorry," Peter said, hoping to be mistaken for a polite person. "I'll bring him back."

"Never mind," Jill said. "We have to finish this interrogation or something really bad will happen."

"And I'm really, really hungry," Sue said hungrily.

"So who's turn was it?" Ann asked.

Sue cleared her throat and looked away. "We can't resume until a certain party moves on."

"Do you think he knows we're talking about him?" Jill asked.

Ann looked Peter up and down. "Not that smart."

"I think I know when I'm not wanted," Peter said, and turned.

"We're not talking about you," Jill whispered. With a nod she pointed behind their bench.

Peter shifted around to see an old man crouching gnome-like behind them. He looked up at Peter, wizened and glowering, upper lip curled back to reveal long, yellow teeth. "Thanks, asshole." His voice was like sandpaper on leather. "What am I going to tell my boss?"

"Tell him you need a younger partner," Peter said momentarily curious.

"Like you?"

"I could use the work," Peter said.

Jill said, "Could you two keep it down, we're trying to sleep." Peter looked over and discovered their heads tipped together eyes shut.

The old man stood and limped away. "Those babes are as much fun as a paper napkin."

"I'll be the judge of that," Peter said, but the old man had already gone.

When Peter turned back the women's eyes were open and they huddled together muttering. Peter stood to one side waiting until one turned to look at him. "You still here?" Jill asked.

"I guess I must be," Peter said, grinning his most charming grin.

To Sue, Ann said, "Should we kill him?"

"Do you think he knows enough to be worth killing?" Sue asked.

"Attention span of a gnat," Ann grumbled. Peter was unaccountably charmed by the pink .38 with gold trim laying seductively in her lap. A very cute gun, he thought, maybe even too cute to shoot.

"Cute because it's pink, or because it's in my lap?" Ann asked defiantly.

"If I said it was cute, I meant it in a military way," Peter responded trying to remember when he'd said it.

"See!" Sue said brightly to Peter. "We're pretty good interrogators."

"And since you don't know anything," Ann added, "this interrogation has come to a premature climax."

For a reason he could neither grasp nor ignore, Peter felt insulted. "I do know a few things. So, when does the interrogation begin?"

"I just told you it's over," Sue said. "We're finished. And we didn't have to ask you a single question."

A dejected Peter looked around to see that the blue dog was back with a dead baby in its jaws.

"Drop that!" Jill said firmly. The dog's mouth opened, the bundle dropped to the ground. Peter was relieved to realize that it was only a plastic doll.

"He does that," Ann said unprompted. "Steals, if you get my meaning."

"We've tried to break him," Sue added.

"He does it for the attention," Jill said.

"You mean, being blue just doesn't do it for him?"

Sue said, "Some dogs just can't get enough attention. Like some people."

"Fuck off!" the blue dog said.

Jill said to Peter, "Foul language is a form of obfuscational obscurantisim. He uses it for even more attention."

"By the way," Jill said turning to the others, "don't we have a bathroom to re-tile or something?"

"We did that yesterday," Sue said. "Today we're supposed to paint the swimming pool."

"Oh, not again," Jill said with a bemused expression. "Didn't we do that last month?"

Peter said, "I'm very good at painting," but the women did not seem to be listening.

To Peter, the blue dog said, "These babes can natter on 'til daybreak and never get anywhere."

"I'm beginning to see your point."

Jill said to Peter, "Taking advice from dogs? How's that working for you?"

The blue dog said, "Better than taking advice from humans."

"Yeah," Sue said. "I can tell its working great!"

"Leave the guy alone," the blue dog said. "He probably wants to take you seriously."

Ann stood, "We'll do better than that." Turning to the other women she asked, "Shall we go?" In response, they stood. "Let's pretend it's getting late, and we still have that outhouse to re-roof."

"You know," Peter said, "I'm good at that, too."

Jill stopped and then turned to Sue and Ann with an uncomfortable frown. "Well, what do you think?"

Sue asked Peter, "How are you on a ladder?"

"Courageous," Peter said. His knees trembled remembering his last roof job and the disaster that ensued.

"Might as well take him," Ann said. "I hate ladder-work. And you two aren't much better."

Peter looked up to notice a man approaching. Tall, slim and broad-shouldered, he wore a wide-brimmed black hat, a long black leather coat and sunglasses. Peter asked, "You know that guy?"

Ann urgently muttered, "Don't look at him." The three women turned their backs on the approaching man.

Peter turned with them. "What's up?" he whispered.

"Wannabes," Sue said smirking. "They're everywhere."

"Wannabe whats?" Peter asked, suddenly feeling as if he was finally about to resolve the mystery. Ann opened her mouth to respond but with a gesture Sue hushed her.

The man reached them and asked, "What's the assignment?"

Peter and the three women turned. Grimfaced and hands shoved deep into his pockets, the man reminded Peter of a large, angular bug. Jill smiled brightly. "Why Gary, how are you?"

"Yeah," Sue said, "it's been almost a whole day."

Gary pursed lips thin as razorblades. "I assume the zircon has been delivered to Fappa."

Ann glanced at Sue and Jill. "Dropped off two nights ago."

"So," Gary asked, "payment for my efforts soon will be forthcoming?"

"Terms of payment," Jill said, "are still being negotiated."

Gary said, "This can't be good." In profile, his face reminded Peter of a tree struck by lightning.

Peter said, "I'd like to introduce myself. I'm Peter." He offered his hand, but Gary did not even turn in his direction.

Ann said to Gary, "He brought the dog back."

Gary asked, "You mean you haven't killed him yet?"

"We've explained this before, Gary," Jill said, her voice dripping exasperation.

"Not every explanation is a justification," Gary said.

Peter asked, "What have you got against the dog?"

Gary finally turned to Peter, "Who's talking about dogs?" He looked Peter up and down and his razorblade lips rippled. Turning back to the women he asked, "How long will it take him to go away?"

"That's pretty rude," Ann said. "You want to listen to yourself once in a while."

To no one in particular Gary said, "I only come here for my assignments. Got anything new for me?"

"We've told you before," Ann said, "we really don't exactly need your help."

Without looking at Peter, Gary asked "So what's he still doing here?"

"We have this roof problem," Sue said quickly, "and he has experience. We know you won't help us with our roof," she said winking in Peter's direction.

"Yeah," Jill added, "you know how many holes we have in our roof."

"Our roof is almost not a roof," Ann said, "what with all the holes."

Gary turned to Peter. "You're going to do something for their roof?"

"Sure," Peter said, relieved he understood nothing. "I've worked roofs for years. Roofs are my friends."

Gary again looked him up and down. "Seems unlikely," he said and then turned to Ann. "I've got to be someplace." He turned and walked slowly away.

"So what's he got against your dog?" Peter asked when Gary was out of earshot.

"You must be one of those question-guys," Sue said with a broad smile. "You have lots of them and they're always good."

"Does that mean you're one of those answer-girls?" Peter asked just as brightly. "Because there's nothing more a question-guy likes than an answer-girl."

"Well," Jill said, "it seems you're shit out of luck today."

Looking around Peter said, "Maybe the dog can help me. By the way, where is your dog?"

Jill said, "Probably gone back to headquarters." Then quickly she added, "I mean, the apartment."

"Wait," Peter said. "I thought you had an outhouse with a roof problem."

"Oh, we do!" Jill insisted. "But we don't actually use it as an outhouse, if you get my point."

Sue added, "It's an outhouse for storing our spy-stuff."

Ann said, "We have spy-stuff we need to store, so we keep it in this outhouse with a leaky roof."

To the others Sue said, "We should leave while there's still daylight so we can show what's-his-name the holes."

"Peter," Peter said. "The name's Peter."

"Of course," Jill said, "we knew that. We were just testing you."

"Testing me?"

"To make sure you aren't a wannabe."

"Wannabe what?"

"Exactly," Ann added. "Now I think we should go."

Peter pretended he knew all about roofs and leaks and questions and their answers, and even about dogs, although if confronted he would have admitted he knew very little about dogs who talk. And since these women with their mysteries were more than sufficiently interesting, Peter, as a true and adventurous question-guy, suspended his disbelief long enough to tolerate not having his questions answered.

The women walked quite a long way. Peter walked with them, sometimes in front and sometimes not, sometimes walking beside Ann and sometimes Jill and still other times beside Sue. They walked along green and leafy streets, and past colorfully festooned buildings, sometimes heading north and other times not. Peter wondered if these women were attempting to confuse him, because he suspected they walked past the same buildings several times. And besides, he had certainly become confused. Peter looked around for the blue dog, but the dog had still not returned. Eventually they approached a fairly new and well-kept apartment building many stories tall.

At the front door, Jill said to Peter, "Let's go up. The key to the outhouse is upstairs."

Peter asked, "And where's the outhouse?"

"Oh, not far away," Ann said.

"Not far at all," Sue said with forced indifference.

Jill said, "We only need to go up for a minute."

They walked to an elevator at the end of the lobby. Crammed together in the elevator's narrow space, Peter was conscious of all of the breasts pressing against his body, a sensation he found pleasantly distracting. To Peter's disappointment, the elevator door eventually opened. They walked the length of a long hallway to a door at the very end. Jill used several keys to unlock several locks until suddenly the door opened.

The apartment they entered was spacious with high ceilings, but what struck Peter was the enormous collection of electronic equipment it contained. He identified computers and transmitters and receivers, but the functions of most of the equipment were beyond his recognition.

Sue turned to Peter with a smile of pride. "We were so lucky to get this place." She avoided looking at the haphazard display of equipment. "And the rent is real reasonable."

The women seemed determined to put Peter at his ease, which simply made him more nervous. "So we'll get the key and go?" he asked hopefully.

"Oh sure," Jill said. "I just need to change into some work clothes. It'll just take me a minute." Then she disappeared through a doorway.

When Jill was gone, Ann asked Peter, "Are you hungry?"

Before Peter could answer, Sue said, "We should have something to eat before we leave for the outhouse."

Peter said, "As long as it doesn't delay getting us there." He didn't want to spoil this new adventure and its opportunity for him to demonstrate several of his virtues.

Sue laughed. "Those holes aren't going anywhere." Ann joined her, until both laughed so long and hard that Peter wondered what it was he had just been told.

Jill reappeared suddenly, and she was definitely not dressed for long travel in any chilly climates. She asked, "Did one of you move the key? Because I can't find it."

Sue said, "Got yourself dressed for some heavy lifting, I see." Then she added, "Ann wants to put together something to eat. Let's look for the key after dinner."

"Sounds great," Jill said. "I'm famished."

Peter suddenly heard scratching at the door. The women pretended to hear nothing, but Peter's curiosity forced him to open it. The blue dog sat at the threshold obviously bruised, scratched and cut-up. And one of his eyes was black. "What happened to you?" Peter asked, already assuming he had asked another question that would never be answered.

"Ask them," the blue dog said, indicating the women with a tip of his chin.

"Why us?" Sue asked. "What could we know?"

The blue dog said, "You sent Gary after me, didn't you?" His question seemed to Peter rhetorical.

"We did no such thing!" Ann said. "Why would we do that?"

"Everybody outlives their usefulness eventually."

"If we wanted to be rid of you," Sue said, "we'd have dragged you to the vet."

"And how many times have I heard that?" the blue dog said. He sauntered to the dog bowls squatting beside the door to the kitchen. Looking back at Peter the blue dog said, "Just remember; everybody gets replaced." Then he noisily lapped his water.

"That's so true," Peter said quickly though to no one in particular.

"Never mind him," Ann said to Peter. "He's just a talking dog who never knows when to shut up."

"You mean," the blue dog said, "I won't let you shut me up."

Ann said, "Seems you have a serious problem shutting yourself up."

"Don't argue with him, Ann," Jill said. "You know that's what he wants."

"What I want," the blue dog said, "is food and sex, and looking around I see none of either."

"Okay, that's enough," Jill said and stood. "One more crack and you'll spend the night in the dumpster."

"Oooooo!" the blue dog said between laps of water, "I'm so scared!"

Jill said, "If you were as smart as you are mouthy, you would be."

"You're one to talk about smart and mouthy."

Peter broke in. "Domestic bliss is charming to witness, but I came up here for the key to the outhouse with the roof that needs to be fixed."

"You know," Jill said glancing out the window, "the light's fading and I'm beginning to think we'd be better off doing this tomorrow."

"Yeah, right," the blue dog said to the wall.

"And besides," Jill said, "dinner's almost ready. Let's have something to eat."

"Hey dimwit," the blue dog called out seemingly to no one as it sauntered through a doorway and out of the room. "Ask them about all this equipment."

Ann and Sue turned to each other and laughed nervously.

Leading the way into the kitchen, Jill said, "Come along and sit down." In a corner of the kitchen stood a circular table hardly larger than a postage stamp; the four chairs around it almost touched each other. They all sat down together elbow to elbow. Jill put a large glass bowl of pretzels and another of potato chips on the table, and beside them a large bottle of purple soda. With withering enthusiasm Jill said, "Dig in!"

The three women began frantically scooping handfuls of pretzels and potato chips into their mouths, and guzzling large quantities of purple soda directly from the bottle that they passed from hand to hand. Peter found the noises they made as they ate quite stimulating. He was so impressed by what he witnessed he forgot to eat. But they all sat so close together that when his neighbors leaned forward, Peter had no choice but to lean forward with them. Peter spoke from the center of his perplexity. "Is any of this going to get us anywhere?"

All three faces turned suddenly to look at him. "Just where," Jill asked, genuinely befuddled, "are any of us trying to get to?"

"Roofs," Peter said, "remember?"

Sue turned to Ann. "That's what I like; focus and tenacity."

"Too bad it's all wasted," Ann responded.

To Peter, Jill said, "Relax and have something to eat."

Peter found himself wondering. "This is not the adventure I had looked forward to."

"See," Ann said to Jill, "we've disappointed him."

"Well," Peter said, now embarrassed by his admission, "I wouldn't put it quite that way."

"And now," Sue said to Ann, "we've embarrassed him by noticing his embarrassment."

"That's not it either," Peter said with a casual swagger. "I'm just wondering when the adventure will begin. Any thoughts?" His consternation was acute. He could not decide if he was more likely to find the adventure he'd left his apartment that morning to find somewhere else, or if he should hang on here a while longer. For the first time that day, he really wanted a dog he could talk to. And just then, the blue dog returned to the kitchen.

"My dog-sense tells me things are going wrong here," the blue dog said slouching toward his water bowl, "and I like to watch."

"Alarmist!" Jill said.

"Listen," Peter said to the blue dog, "I'm in a quandary here."

The dog sneezed. "Is that what they call it these days?"

"Stick a plug in it!" Jill said. "The man means to ask you a question."

"Really," Peter pleaded, "all I want to know is whether this is all there is. That's all."

The silence that followed was thick as dark green jelly. It seemed to Peter that they all suddenly had frozen in place. Like bugs in amber there was neither forward nor backward, neither past nor future. The Park suddenly seemed a distant memory, and then more like something glimpsed in a dream. The women seated around the table became increasingly familiar; as if Peter was gradually recalling their pasts in a world within which talking blue dogs were principle actors, and secret agents were undifferentiated elements of a broader paranoia. Peter found himself considering paths, how they appear, whether they are created or simply discovered, and how they achieve materiality. Were paths added to or subtracted from this world? Or were paths as unlikely as talking blue dogs?

Peter was annoyed that his questions were not products of idle yet conscious speculation, but instead squirted out unwilled from a grappling confusion and onto an unevenly liquid surface, mere anchors made of paper and dreams. These women were as charming as Peter could want, perhaps more charming than he could endure. And he recognized their charm as a deliciously sweet net, a glittering cotton-candy gossamer web, a cloud of stringy sweet air. Maybe the dog has it right. Maybe the nattering, chattering, chirping intensity of their voices, separate and apart from the words and their meanings, cast an entrapping seduction. Perhaps he had been ensnared by the illusion that if only he listened long enough and closely enough, something important would be revealed.

Or perhaps it was their exchanges, as if voices responded to voices, each voice assuring that the others must exist. He was no longer certain that words and their thoughts implied each other.

The Park had provided a base from which Peter could extrapolate a reality, a material terrain of suggestive expectations, aspirations indigenous rather than imported. Its paths had led only to other paths, as if the purpose of the Park was to offer a maze of paths without end, simply to demonstrate that all is connected at some level, and any perception of discontinuity is simply the failure to discern connections. And the talking blue dog? Could the dog be a messenger from Peter to himself? Was the talking blue dog simply asking the questions Peter could not ask himself? An alter-ego, a contrapuntal resonating voice for Peter's delusional constructs? As if Peter had unconsciously assembled these parts to satisfy a curiosity of what the whole might resemble if it existed, and then provide a dry-run for a reality Peter could only hope existed. An exercise in self-indulgence? This phenomenon is not unknown to Peter, he's been here before, if that's where he is. And he expects to be here again, if here is where he will be.

There is only so much variety in reality, limits are frequent and appear everywhere. If Peter could save this illusion in a jar, he could put the jar on a shelf next to all those other jars containing all of his other illusions; Peter's Encyclopedic Library of Illusions. He thinks that the perfect profession for him would be illusion-taxidermist. He imagines himself in a silent room surrounded by illusions stuffed and mounted into lifelike postures revealing the true nature and character of themselves. Peter likes this idea; it makes him smile since it even allows for talking blue dogs.

The answer to that question demands a deeper mind than Peter's, and he is relieved to concede this. What he cannot recognize is that the talking blue dog's presence offers an appearance of interconnectedness that ties the illusion of female secret agents to the illusion of intentionality. Peter sits with his chin on his fist waiting for something to be affirmed. All illusions must be grounded by some reference to some reality, and even a talking blue dog is simply a dog.

Peter leans back on his park bench with the sun warming his face as children play noisily nearby, while further off, the sound of a siren cuts the air and then fades. Peter concludes that this was not such a great adventure. But he resolves to visit the Park again. It's always possible, given the nature of the Park, that the next adventure will be better than this one. He looks about pleased that this is that kind of Park. Never the same twice, there's always a chance it will be a better Park tomorrow.

THE FINAL DEATH OF ROCK-AND-ROLL

I WAS IN LONDON at Christmas in 1970. The friend I was staying with walked me around to the hotel Hendrix had been staying at when he od'd. As we approached the building we passed a man who looked remarkably like my senior-year high school history teacher, and he carried a copy of Catcher In The Rye. Except that this man had one arm. I said to my friend, "Who is that one-armed man?" But my friend didn't glance. The man caught me watching him and in a moment he was gone, so my friend and I went into the hotel bar.

Over the years I've wondered about that one-armed man. Even now it seems such a fugitive moment. And I've wondered if, in the final analysis, he could be blamed for the death of rock-and-roll.

In the hotel bar a woman introduced herself to us as Maryann Faithful. The fact that she was a large, middle-aged, dark-haired woman who spoke with a flowery Scottish accent did not seem to bother her. Though neither of us had ever met Maryann Faithful, my friend and I both suspected this woman was not who she claimed to be. But with a dismissive laugh she offered to buy us both a drink for the holiday and promised she'd introduce us to some of her rock-star friends. My friend and I were suddenly very thirsty.

As the three of us sat down together at the bar I looked around the room. A man who looked a lot like Jeff Beck was having lunch at a table tucked into a shadowy corner with someone who looked remarkably like Ginger Baker, and they were being served by a man who looked surprisingly like Joe Cocker. These men suddenly looked at me as if they knew what I was thinking. But that, of course, was impossible since I wasn't thinking anything except why they weren't out saving rock-and-roll. Didn't they even really care? My confusion was painful, but the avalanche of doubt in the dedication of well-known rock-and-roll artists all but overwhelmed me. Could the salvation of rock- and-roll be all finally up to me? Though it was near Christmas I did not feel jolly. This was not my idea of a great way to spend this charming holiday.

Over our drinks, Maryann Faithful asked if we would like to meet Frank Zappa, and of course my friend and I both got pretty excited. With a sly grin Maryann Faithful said, "Such a thing could be arranged. I know you are on a crusade and I believe I can help you save rock-and-roll." She clutched my forearm until it hurt like hell and I had to twist it away from her. "I have friends," she whispered hotly. "They will know what to do." My friend was skeptical but I saw the advantages immediately.

Between many toasts to the upcoming holiday, Maryann Faithful promised to take us to a house in the woods where Stevie Winwood and the members of Traffic lived and had their pictures taken and got high with their girlfriends. She assured us Traffic would be on our side, surely they would save rock-and-roll. Since we'd become fairly drunk, my friend and I agreed to visit them.

Riding in her silly English automobile, Maryann Faithful drove us into the middle of some woods to a painfully dilapidated cottage, only to discover that Stevie Winwood and the members of Traffic were off on-tour in the US. And worse, their girlfriends had gone with them. Maryann Faithful had a key and let us into the house where she fixed us more drinks. Then she said she had forgotten something and had to leave, but that she'd be right back. Before either of us could stop her she was gone. That's how my friend and I became stranded, marooned and abandoned in the heart of England.

We mulled over alternative courses of action for awhile when Maryann Faithful suddenly returned. With her was a large young woman. Blond with large, starry-blue eyes and a bigger smile, she wore a red dress that fit her like a coating of varnish. There was no point to disguise, she was indeed a large, smiling woman and her name was Trudy. With a slight and thoroughly thrilling lisp Trudy said, "I most earnestly wish to, like, help and whatever with the salvation of rock-and-roll and all forms of, like, indigenous music of the people. Wanna smoke some dope?"

Maryann Faithful said to us, "I need to make some phone calls." She sat down by the phone and brought out her phone book. "I think I know where I can find Mick Jagger and Keith Richards. They'll help you save rock-and-roll, I'm sure of it."

"How about John Lennon?" I asked hopefully.

Maryann Faithful shook her head saying that was more impossible than Jimi Hendrix. But then her smile returned. "Why don't you three go in that other room and amuse yourselves while I make these calls. Who knows? Maybe I can get Rod Stewart, or even John Mayall? They would help you, too."

"What about the Bonzo Dog Band?" I asked.

Maryann Faithful's expression darkened. If she had been weather, we would have been up to our hips in a blizzard. "There isn't any Bonzo Dog Band," she said through clenched teeth. "Just a pick-up band of has-beens from the London Philharmonic. And they don't even write their own music."

I told her I was disappointed to hear this, and conceded that maybe their assistance would not be necessary for the salvation of rock-and-roll. My assurance worked; the snow and ice melted, in an instant her weather changed back to a bright Christmas sunshine.

The big smiling girl named Trudy made her smile so big it filled the room edge to edge. My friend and I had to step around it. Maryann Faithful turned to her saying, "Run along with these boys and see if you can help them out." Then she opened her phone book and picked up the receiver.

Trudy said, "The salvation of rock-and-roll is a foregone conclusion." This might have been some secret signal but I never found out. We adjourned in embarrassed confusion to the room Maryann Faithful had suggested.

At the center of this room was a bed the size of a small pond. To me looking at it, it seemed like it was a hot and hazy afternoon in July and the pond was saying, "What are doing with all those clothes on? C'mon in." Trudy's apparel wasn't nearly as difficult to remove as a coating of varnish. Unsheathed she was even more generously formed, a grandly proportioned symphony in flesh. Had she been a house, my friend and I each would have had our own floor. To our delight, Trudy invited us to explore.

We wandered in rooms and looked out windows, we peered in closets and passed through hallways, we climbed up to the attic and even checked out the cellar. After one particularly exhausting climb I stepped out of the pond and wandered into the next room. Maryann Faithful was still on the phone, but now she was speaking to someone in German. This did not upset me as I do not speak that language and so had no idea what she was saying. I returned to our exploration. It was only later, while my friend and I were playing table-tennis on Trudy's back patio, that we all heard a car's motor suddenly rev and then the grind of rubber on crushed stone. And just as suddenly, there we were, abandoned again in the middle of nowhere lost in Trudy's mansion and with the salvation of rock-and-roll in the balance.

For the first time Trudy appeared distressed. She said, "You must return to London if you're going to save rock-and-roll," thus sharing a well-shaped perception. Now I realize that she was more right than I could have guessed.

Donning garments less transparent but just as pervious to the cold, the three of us left the cottage and walked to the edge of a narrow country road hoping to flag a ride back to London. Though we were isolated in the heart of nowhere surrounded with trees and whatever else stood beside this little road, almost instantly a van appeared. The van was covered with wildly-colored images. Painted everywhere were flowers and birds and recording contracts and residual schedules. This was clearly an opportunity to travel with rock-and-roll compatriots to London and foment a revolution from within. The van seemed about to pass us by, until Trudy stepped forward and waved. The van skidded in the gravel to a halt. My friend and I were more relieved than surprised.

Trudy got into the van first. Despite, or perhaps because of, her generous proportions her entrance was greeted with wild huzzahs. It was a tight fit, what with all the rock-and-rollers the van already contained. When my friend and I entered however, we were not greeted with huzzahs. More like an irritated silence. Trudy filled the van with her inviting smile, excursions and forays were organized by enthusiastic volunteers to explore her nooks and crannies. With songs of praise Trudy encouraged deep explorations and broad surveys. When the prime territories had been divided up, my friend and I were left only with a few opportunities for side-trips. The van rocked as it rolled, a true rock-and-roll vehicle, the result of all the coming and going over Trudy's terrain and the enthusiasm thereby stimulated.

Suddenly the van screeched to a stop. Looking out I discovered there was a car parked to block our progress. Although it was night and dark as the inside of a grape, standing in the car's headlights I recognized Maryann Faithful. She signaled to our van frantically waving her arms. The driver of the van ordered us out. All except Trudy, who still possessed sites that demanded exploration.

My friend and I resisted our expulsion, but a sound thrashing delivered by the remaining rock-and-roll explorers finally put us right.

With heavy hearts my friend and I watched the red eyes of the tail-lights of the rocking-and-rolling van recede and then blink out, the cold and damp around us thereby becoming colder and damper. But even before the van disappeared into the black maw of the night, Maryann Faithful had already hustled us into her car. She said, "We have an appointment with Rod Argent. He is between unprofitable tours and has agreed to make his sage advice available to you at a nominal charge."

My friend and I had hoped to reserve our funds for expenditures more directly related to the salvation of rock-and-roll, or for more famous rock-stars. But Maryann Faithful had her own ideas.

We drove almost until dawn in directions I could no longer discern. Finally in the pearl blue light of approaching daybreak, we drove up to a squat, grey cinderblock bungalow in the heart of a working-class suburb of Somerset. The bungalow was painted as grey as anything I've ever seen, and even more grey than its neighbors. It could have been the greyest house in Somerset.

In response to our knock at the front door a squat grey man appeared. Where he wasn't bald, lank black hair fringed his mud-grey face. Behind that hair he could have been having a piano recital, or perhaps a theatrical performance, the black fringe was that long and that dense. Maryann Faithful introduced us as crusaders in the name of rock-and-roll. The man introduced to us as Rod Argent grimaced as he looked us over. I waited for him to say there had been a mistake, and he was in fact Rod Argent the business accountant from Bristol. If his expression had been a saw, my friend and I would have been cut in numerous small sections. Maryann Faithful pushed past us making a big deal about how great it was to see him again. With the grace of a ballet- dancer she hooked Rod Argent's arm in her own and steered him inside. My friend and I followed as if we had an alternative.

Standing in Rod Argent's living room, Rod Argent glowered. "You boys need a hobby. You've got too bloody much time on your hands, if you ask me." I told him that when rock-and-roll was saved, hobbies would be abolished. My friend was impressed by my sagacity, but he was a majority of one. Maryann Faithful disappeared into the back of the house, leaving my friend and I to confront this scowling version of Rod Argent.

To dispel the grim fog threatening to fill the room, my friend asked Rod

Argent how his last tour had gone. His scowl turned into a grimace when he replied that he would have made a lot more money if only people would show up when he played. He said he was tired of playing to packed houses of dogs and cats. He said he didn't mind them as an audience. They respond with remarkable enthusiasm for audiences that can't clap their hands and whistle. But they never buy his t-shirts, which is where he and most rock-and-rollers make most of their money. How can I make any money, he asked, if the audience don't buy the bloody t-shirts? What's the bloody use of having bloody fans what don't buy your bloody t-shirts?

My friend and I were both stumped by that one. I expressed dismay at the lowly state of rock-and-roll, and my friend nodded in sympathetic agreement. After a silence that could have been a mountain, my friend asked how Rod Argent's most recent album was selling. His eyebrows rose like suspenders in the dark, apparently the question caught him by surprise. Just then, Maryann Faithful returned carrying a tray of cheese sandwiches.

"You boys must be hungry," she said. "These are special cheese sandwiches my mother taught me to make, especially spiced with squirrel innards and orange peels. It's an English specialty." She set the tray on a small table.

"I've just been asked how my latest album is selling," Rod Argent reported to Maryann Faithful. "How should I respond?" His tiny black eyes were bright with curiosity.

Maryann Faithful thought for a moment. Then she smiled. "Well!" she said. "The appropriate answer to that question is that your albums are selling well. In fact, you might add that they are selling very well, indeed."

This seemed to confuse Rod Argent. If his confusion had been soup, it would have been more like mashed potatoes, but not as yellow. An uncomfortable silence followed. Only Maryann Faithful seemed to know how to eat these peculiar sandwiches. My friend suddenly said he was pleased to hear that Rod Argent's album was selling well because it deserved to sell well. He was convinced it was a particular and unique type of well-selling album. This seemed to dispel the miasma that had begun to descend from the ceiling like a badly tattered curtain. Even Rod Argent felt constrained to smile, not a pretty sight in the daylight.

Maryann Faithful devoured one sandwich and then another. My friend and I suffered an anxious moment since neither of us was sure how one best consumed these sandwiches. English food is so much like this, there's no point to discussion. She finally noticed there were almost as many sandwiches on the platter as there had been when she put them out. This caused her some concern. With a smile she said that whoever finished the most sandwiches would get a nice surprise. My friend and I were confused by this, but Rod Argent suddenly began to consume the sandwiches as though they were made of air and flavored by sunshine.

She took enormous pleasure at the sight of Rod Argent eating her sandwiches. She turned to us shaking her head. The look in her eyes said that we would regret forever the loss of this opportunity to sample authentic English cuisine. A pang of guilt thrust its pointed shaft through my heart, but that did not help me in eating those sandwiches. My friend seemed to be suffering the same discomfort but neither of us said anything. Soon there was only one sandwich remaining on the platter.

Maryann Faithful and Rod Argent stared at each other over that last sandwich; a battle of minds was taking place behind their eyes. Suddenly Rod Argent snatched the last sandwich from the platter and stuffed it into his mouth before she could grab it. Rod Argent seemed to believe he had won, but Maryann Faithful reached into his mouth and grabbed the sandwich back, pushed it between her own lips and swallowed before any of us could react. A remarkable come-back for a rapidly-fading pop singer.

She leaned back grinning with an expression of victory, a look of historical inevitability, a smile of complacent superiority. Then, while my friend and I endured a confusing sensation of loss, Maryann Faithful stood from our table. To Rod Argent she said, "This is obviously your lucky day."

Rod Argent asked, "Was that something you learned in Viet-Nam?" But then, as if a small eruption of the scent of honeysuckle had blossomed in his mind, Rod Argent smiled and stood. "Suddenly I sure hope so."

Maryann Faithful led as if she knew the way. Rod Argent followed her at a remarkably close proximity until they disappeared through a door. There were voices and then laughter, but the sound warped, delayed and then rearranged itself as it passed through the brick and stone walls so that it sounded like a guitar solo.

Not a very good solo, my friend and I both agreed. It got better when the drums kicked in, but it went on a long time. We became tired of staring at the empty tray so we stared out the window. When we got tired of looking out the window we concluded that our crusade was not going well. We were as far as ever from the salvation of rock-and- roll. So we left.

We agreed that if we could find a really big highway, like the M-1 or something, we might at least get back to London. So we began to walk. We walked south confident we would soon find a really big highway. Because the really big highways always have trucks traveling them going to London. My friend explained all this to me as we walked freezing in the coagulated December evening. My friend expressed absolute certainty that the moment we found a really big highway, we were home. So we walked.

We walked a long time. We walked for such a long time that I had to sit down. England did not appear to be this big on a map. We had yet to spot even a sign pointing to any big highways. If highways were trees, this was a desert. We seemed to be caught in the English Highway Desert. My friend insisted he knew where we were, but a breath of skepticism brushed my cheek.

The more the daylight faded, the fewer people and houses we saw. It was as if the light and the people came packaged together. As if the English people were like fireflies and carried their own light. It is a terrible thing when skepticism degenerates into anxiety. Cold and anxious and lost in the middle of the Great English Highway Desert. Suddenly I would have exchanged my burial plot for a bite of one of those cheese-and- squirrel innards-and-orange peel sandwiches. My friend warned me that if I fell by the roadside, my carcass would be devoured by predators. I laughed and asked if he expected me to believe there were lions or tigers in Dorset. But my friend stopped suddenly, turned and looked so deeply into my eyes I wondered if his sight had penetrated to the back of my head. He said that strange things lurk in England. While the place looks like a really big garden, he said, even in a really big garden bad things happen and creepy creatures lurk.

I wasn't really scared, but I wasn't really happy either. The cost of saving rock- and-roll was going up faster than the price of heroin. And now the sky was as dark as night, which was both frightening but also reassuring, since it was night. We were about as alone as we could be in a desert without trees or really big highways. I was thinking that being without either a highway or a tree put us in a terrible position for the salvation of rock-and-roll, when suddenly at the edge of the horizon a pair of bright headlights appeared. Somehow I was able to recognize we were now in very serious trouble. But by the time we had begun to run away, the car was right there in front of us.

The front door opened. The man behind the wheel said, "I say; are you the chaps who are trying to save rock-and-roll?" He was a large man—no, make that a huge man—wearing a dark blue suit and a white shirt and a red-orange tie. He was so big he did not stand up, he just turned with one tree-size leg extending out the car door. His huge-man's pink face framed a smile as cheap as a thrift-store coffee pot. In place of hair he wore a dark brown rayon wig. In the light from his car, the wig looked piled up on his head and about to tip over. He gazed up at us expectantly. Unfortunately, there didn't seem a good answer to his question that wasn't the truth. We stood, and he sat, for some time. I searched for a lie that was better than the truth. If it appeared, in the darkness I must have missed it.

The pressure weighed on all of us, a sense of inevitable disaster. This encounter had begun badly and was getting worse. The man's small dark eyes seemed to want to hide in his face-pockets for the shame and despair they felt for their owner. Even this man in his car recognized that something had gone wrong. But suddenly and unprompted he said, "I suppose I should say something like, good evening, my name is John Entwhistle, and Maryann Faithful sent me."

Even though it was still night, it was as if the sun had come out. John Entwhistle said that if we got into his car, he would take us to a place where we would reunite with Maryann Faithful. My friend's glance clouded, his face was as hostile as a darkened tv. As if seeing this without looking, John Entwhistle went on to explain how upset Maryann Faithful was about the pending doom of rock-and-roll, and that she had enlisted quite a number of prominent English musicians in her cause. There was no doubt, rock-stars were becoming concerned. Oddly enough this assurance was sufficient. My friend and I got into the car, John Entwhistle turned it around and we were off.

Though he had an annoying, high-pitched, fat-man's voice, he could talk a lot. He could talk the light out of a light bulb. My friend and I listened to tale after anecdote about various well-known rock celebrities. I wish I could remember just one. I'm sure they were funny. But by this time, the night had become a stew and its events blended and mixed with the brown sauce of futility. Exhaustion descended on me like a meal of bad stew. Combined with the hum of the highway, the drone of the bass player for the Who flicked off my lights. This I do remember.

When I woke up we were driving through a town I did not recognize. The sky was a pre-dawn violet, or something very close. My friend had managed to stay awake. John Entwhistle was just finishing a tale involving Mick Jagger and John Cage that must have been very amusing. Even my friend was smiling, something I had not seen since Trudy's arrival. When John Entwhistle saw that I was awake he said, "Just thought you'd like to know, the house we're going to once belonged to Richard Harris. You know; Mister MacArthur Park?"

For a moment I was angry. Only the very lamely unhip didn't know MacArthur Park. Why would the bass player for the Who think that an American crusader for the salvation of rock-and-roll wouldn't know MacArthur Park? But the English must be excused, or so I tried to remind myself. After all, they didn't invent rock-and-roll, they just made a lot of money at it.

The sky continued to lighten in a powdery pink-blue, and now I could see we were driving through a suburban housing development that could have been a patch of the good old USA. Inexplicably this sight left me moved. Not only was saving rock-and- roll turning out to be tough, it was also lonely. Even with my friend's companionship, the burden of home-sickness grew on my back like a festering boil. And after forty-eight hours we seemed no closer to a solution to the dilemma confronting the most popular music in the world. My heart had become a leaky bucket, my confidence had begun to puddle at my feet. This was no longer a joke, if it ever had been.

The housing development we entered was as featureless as a teenager's soul. John Entwhistle piloted us through a series of turns that baffled me. The development's deficiency of landmarks tempted me to suspect we might just as well be driving in circles. But he continued ahead with remarkable unconcern, as if he could have driven this route with his eyes welded shut.

Finally, as the tip of the sun's nose had just exposed itself between two one-story bungalows, we pulled into a driveway. This house appeared identical to every other within a wide area, and only the red bicycle lying across the concrete path to the front door seemed to make it unique. When I pointed this out to John Entwhistle he simply laughed saying that almost every homeowner in England now artistically positions a red bicycle across the path to their front door. It was simply something residents had picked up from watching American television shows. Not that he had anything against that, he assured me.

Extricating himself from behind the steering wheel took the very large John Entwhistle some time, though he never overtly requested assistance. More as if, before making any movement, he would take a moment to think.

Given the complex gymnastics, this seemed prudent, and my friend and I did not interfere. Eventually completing a series of contortions remarkable for their grace and economy he emerged sporting a broad smile. "Maryann Faithful will be ever so happy to see you again. Your crusade has inspired her, particularly since recently she has sustained certain reversals in her own career. Her dedication to your crusade almost exceeds her enthusiasm; no small thing given her excessive age." With a hand as big as a shovel he slapped my friend and I on the shoulder with a single blow. As if simultaneously being struck by lightning, we both suddenly fell sprawling to the concrete. And we discovered we had tripped over the bicycle.

"Oh dear," John Entwhistle said incapable of leaning forward to help. "This is not beginning well. This could be an omen, a sign of certain ill-fortune. I believe I shall be going now. You young gents will sort it all out I'm sure."

With a display of agility that startled us, John Entwhistle dashed faster than I would have thought that legs like his could take him, opened the car door and then threw himself inside. My friend and I overcame our surprise and began to run after him, but by some apt twist of girth, John Entwhistle positioned himself behind the wheel, got the car wheeling backward at a remarkable speed, spun it cleverly, and then screeched along the curving lane and out of sight. We listened to his vehicle roar long after it disappeared. Along with his departure disappeared the last confetti of hope in my battle to preserve rock-and-roll.

Stranded again, or so it seemed. Every time we had come close to untangling the riddle of the demise of rock-and-roll, its trail went up in smoke. Once again we had been abandoned within sight of our goal. Of the entire crusade, our hearts now reached their lowest point. Though our effort finally appeared futile, if we could not enter this house, we might at least speak with whoever lived there. We stepped around the red bicycle and reached the front door without incident. By now the sun had entirely cleared the horizon and hung complete and exposed in the center of a cloudless sky spreading a crystalline light that etched each surface and contour.

Pressing the doorbell played the first measure of "Winter" from the "Four Seasons" by Antonio Vivaldi. I recognized it from having, as a teenager, been given a well-intended Christmas gift by a relative who misread record labels with remarkable inattention. It took some minutes, but finally we heard sounds of movement behind the door. A brass lock clicked and then the door opened. When the man appeared, my friend and I both unconsciously took one step back.

Suddenly the doorway was filled by a young, slim black man about six feet tall. He was clean-shaven and his head was shaved to the scalp as well, the dark skin of his skull glistened in the brightening daylight. Dressed casually in a brown-red work shirt and blue jeans, he wore wire-rim glasses tinted dark amber and he smoked a cigarette. His appearance was otherwise unremarkable, except that in his right earlobe he wore a sparkling ruby stud the size of a tab of acid.

Very quietly this man asked, "What can I do for you fellows?" There was a quality about his voice that seemed familiar. When neither my friend nor I could think of a response he said, "What is it with you jokers?"

And then I knew. "They say you're dead?"

The man slipped his glasses low on his nose and then surveyed the neighborhood.

With a furtive gesture he ushered us inside and then shut the door. "This is not cool," he said without rancor, almost sympathetic. "Some people can take hints, but apparently that population does not include you. C'mon in and sit for a while before I throw you out."

We followed him up a set of stairs to a large loft-like room. A pair of wide windows at the far-end of the room opened to a large garden behind the house. On an easel against the wall was a large oil-on-canvas painting in progress of a garden. Beside it a half dozen more paintings of various garden scenes leaned against the wall. It was as if the garden continued inside the room. At the far side of the room was a pair of sofas neatly arranged on either side of a low wide table. On one of the sofas perched a plain but charming young black woman. She smiled. The man deferentially addressed her saying, "Lady Ester Hancock-Russell, allow me to introduce to you two music enthusiasts who have washed up upon our shore. With your permission I have invited them to join us for a cup of tea."

Lady Hancock-Russell's smile broadened and she nodded graciously. Her smile was charming, coming as a surprise from an unlikely visage. "But of course, James," she said in a voice as warm and rich as sweet-smelling smoke. Despite her appearance, everything about her was seductive. With four words, I was already half in love with her.

My friend and I sat down. The room was plain, almost without adornment except for the paintings and the obligatory but tasteful scattering of Christmas decorations. As we watched him pour out the tea, Lady Ester commented about the weather and speculated about the new year. When silence again descended, she asked my friend and me about ourselves. As briefly as possible we explained where we had been, but when I broached the subject of the crusade to save rock-and-roll, the man's expression darkened. Following a flurry of obscure gestures I finally realized he wanted me to drop the subject. Smiling, he abruptly stood. To Lady Ester he said, "These young men have come to discuss a matter of considerable urgency. Could you spare us a few moments alone?"

Lady Ester's smile faded. She looked at my friend and me with gradually freezing scorn. If the room had been a meat locker, it would have been just the right temperature. But she turned to the man and regained her smile. "Remember, James, we're having lunch with the Mitchell-Rothmans in an hour." She stood; a gesture of both practiced grace and naive charm. My half-love gave way to adoration. There was a lump in my throat the size of a hashish tennis ball. To my friend and me she said, "Please don't burden James with your disappointments. It is time you became adults. Shoulder your own misery, you're old enough now."

There didn't seem much value to any response to that, though my heart was now breaking for this plain but gorgeous woman. I could only watch as she gracefully disappeared up the stairs without looking back.

The three of us sat enveloped in a silence as cold and wet as an English summer. Despite the chill and damp, a tension gradually built walls between my friend and me and this man. My friend murmured that we had come a long way in hope of his help, and that he couldn't just abandon us like this. I didn't think this was a promising start, but I said nothing.

After some hesitation the man said that he was sorry we had come such a long way, mostly because that meant we would have a long trip back. He insisted that unfortunately there was nothing he could do about the death of rock-and-roll. He regretted the sorry state of popular music, but it was no longer his problem. My heart sank. Coming from this speaker, those words crushed every nerve in my body. As if my skin had been peeled entirely off. For a moment I thought I'd go blind with despair.

Suddenly and without even realizing it I began to speak. "Try to imagine the world without rock-and-roll. A world empty of the spontaneous joy of the boring drum- kick, the sophomoric lyric, the trivial melody, the out-of-tune bass line. It's just as easy to imagine a world without puppy dogs or cigarette papers or smiling young women. Rock-and-roll is as inevitable as the five-fingered hand." My argument drifted and I knew I should stop, but the fate of rock-and-roll was in the balance. Words took possession of my mouth. I had no choice but to continue. My friend was dismayed, and the man in front of us appeared to be falling sleep. But I pressed my case.

"Rock-and-roll allows the future to happen. Rock-and-roll is like the puss from the wound of adolescence. It must come out for the patient to acquire the strength to go on. Without rock-and-roll we will be left without a season of vivifying excess. Without rock-and-roll, youth will be merely a hard and barren moment between the afflictions of childhood and the oppressions of parenthood. The dance must have a rhythm, and the rhythm of the dance is rock-and-roll. Un-danceable life, un-musical life, blind to the rhythms of the body, deaf to the pounding blood. Rock-and-roll is our way of breathing together."

I looked up. Both my friend and the man were gone.

I was left to wonder if I had been too emphatic. Or if I had asked the impossible. I had aligned my arguments like toy soldiers of cut-crystal glass. I had deployed them as best I could in the confusion of battle. And they'd gotten blasted. In an instant they were reduced to glittering and lacerating shards, useless except as trash. Our crusade had failed, rock-and-roll was doomed. My feeble attempt seemed almost to speed that process. There were so many rock stars I had yet to contact, but suddenly it had all revealed itself as useless. I sat for awhile feeling the flow of time that passed by my face as palpably as if I was submerged in surging water. I began making plans to return to America and gather the remaining pieces to salvage what I could. And then from somewhere my friend emerged. He came to stand beside the couch.

"Mr. and Lady Hancock-Russell have left. It's time we got back to London." There was a look about his face that said, wish me luck.

We walked to the crossroads and the bus stop. The air around us seemed filled with a kind of white noise, the sound of a stage-full of guitar amplifiers all turned on and ready to play, a buzzing, hissing sound that fills the blood with anticipation. The man had given my friend enough money for bus-fare and cigarettes to get us back to London. We both knew that eventually I would ask him, so I did.

My friend said, "He said he was sorry that Jimi Hendrix had died, and that he understood how people might take his death very hard. But he said as far as he was concerned, Jimi Hendrix had to die just so that rock-and-roll could die. And he said that rock-and-roll had to die so that it could become perfect and eternal. Rock-and-roll needed to fix itself permanently, freeze itself. He said if Hendrix had stayed around, eventually he would have gotten stale and that would have turned rock-and-roll into a dull-witted cliché. He'd have ended up fat and bald and playing the Las Vegas gambling lounges. The man thought that Hendrix had known exactly what he was doing. As far as he's concerned, he said, Hendrix gave up his life to save rock-and-roll."

I thought about that. We stood in cold, bright sunlight. The sharp breeze and bright light told me that now, finally, things would be better, just as soon as I got home.

On the other side of the highway stretched a field of shorn yellow straw that ended with a stand of black, naked trees. Sunlight poured over every shape etching edges with silver-yellow light, a world dipped into candied violin lacquer. In the distance a large bird flew along the tops of the row of trees and then soared into the chilly, hard blue sky like a great black tear.

I said, "Oh wow. Far-out. That's heavy."

Because at the time, and in that place, all of that seemed sufficient.

A.W. DEANNUNTIS lives in Philadelphia, Pennsylvania and has published fiction in periodicals that include "The Evansville Review" (a recent magazine publication), *Philadelphia Short Stories, Silent Voices, The Armchair Aesthete, Timber Creek Review, Lynx Eye, Los Angeles Review, Yemassee, First Class, Pacific Coast Journal, Short Stories Bimonthly, Luna Negra, CrossConnect, Spout, The Iconoclast, North Atlantic Review, Nite-Writer's International, Onionhead, Nuthouse, Mind in Motion* (Pushcart Prize nomination), *Kiosk, Cimarron Review, California Quarterly, Dog River Review* and *Coe Review*, as well as the novels *Master Siger's Dream* (2011) and *The Mermaid at the Americana Arms Motel* (2011) with What Books Press.

PROSE

Rebbecca Brown, *They Become Her*

François Camoin, *April, May, and So On*

A.W. DeAnnuntis, *Master Siger's Dream*

A.W. DeAnnuntis, *The Final Death of Rock and Roll and Other Stories*

A.W. DeAnnuntis, *The Mermaid at the Americana Arms Motel*

Katharine Haake, *The Origin of Stars and Other Stories*

Katharine Haake, *The Time of Quarantine*

Mona Houghton, *Frottage & Even As We Speak: Two Novellas*

Rod Val Moore, *Brittle Star*

Chuck Rosenthal, *Are We Not There Yet?*
Travels in Nepal, North India, and Bhutan

Chuck Rosenthal, *Coyote O'Donohughe's History of Texas*

Chuck Rosenthal, *West of Eden: A Life in 21st Century Los Angeles*

What Books Press books may be ordered from:
SPDBOOKS.ORG | ORDERS@SPDBOOKS.ORG | (800) 869 7553 | AMAZON.COM

Visit our website at
WHATBOOKSPRESS.COM

www.ingramcontent.com/pod-product-compliance
Lightning Source LLC
Chambersburg PA
CBHW020615120726
47905CB00003B/801